Praise for Lissa Matthews's
Twisted Up

"From the first page, I fell in love with the hot, sexy cowboy who won't take 'no' for an answer... know it's a book that I'll read again, both for the 'Holy smokes! That is SO freaking hot' sex, and for the tender, loving, affectionate relationship that develops between Justin and Ella."

~ *Guilty Pleasures Book Reviews*

"For Lissa Matthews' fans, this story is twisted just enough to see the world of love from a different and to my mind a more realistic perspective than many other authors present. In *Twisted Up* you will find yourself laughing, frowning, aroused, pleased, stressed and ultimately happy. It is definitely a journey worth making."

~ *BlackRaven's Reviews*

Look for these titles by
Lissa Matthews

Now Available:

Pink Buttercream Frosting
Arctic Shift

Blue Jeans and Hard Hats
Sweet Caroline
Cracklin' Rosie

Twisted Up

Lissa Matthews

SAMHAIN PUBLISHING

Samhain Publishing, Ltd.
11821 Mason Montgomery Road, 4B
Cincinnati, OH 45249
www.samhainpublishing.com

Twisted Up
Copyright © 2012 by Lissa Matthews
Print ISBN: 978-1-60928-810-5
Digital ISBN: 978-1-60928-703-0

Cover by Kendra Egert

First Samhain Publishing, Ltd. electronic publication: December 2011
First Samhain Publishing, Ltd. print publication: November 2012

Dedication

To the real Cowboy Justin, for all the inspiration and love you long to share. To Graylin for daily bowls of coffee. To N.D. for bunny slippers and laughter when I think too hard. And to my readers for being patient, for being honest, for helping me get through the wall, brick by brick. Thank you.

Chapter One

"Justin?" Ella gasped. "What are you doing here?"

Justin grinned at his pretty, albeit surprised, lover. "I'm here to get you, Ella."

"Get me?"

"Yep. I'm tired of this long-distance, once-every-few-weeks shit. I'm tired of you canceling on me. This nonsense of you not giving us a chance has to stop." He hadn't meant to say it quite like that before he ever got in the door, but the words just kind of jumped out. He wouldn't take them back.

"It's not nonsense, and I've had to cancel because of work. I told you that. Life has just gotten in the way, that's all."

Did she really believe that? Did she really expect him to believe it? He might have if her gaze hadn't shifted from side to side instead of looking straight at him. "I might be younger than you, but I wasn't born yesterday. I call bullshit."

The blush that stained her cheeks in the early afternoon sun touched him as did the uncertain look in her eyes. He didn't want to make her feel bad, but he wanted her, damn it, and he was going to have her. He'd even come prepared for her resistance, and he was afraid he'd have to pull out all the stops.

"Justin, please, what are you really doing here? And while I'm asking questions, how'd you find out my address?"

"I told you why I'm here. How I got your address, well..." He shrugged, not a bit apologetic. "I called the hotel's home office."

Ella nodded knowingly, finally pinning him with her stare. "And sweet-talked whomever answered the phone into giving you my address, no doubt. Some of those girls hear a sexy twang and would give away their firstborn if asked."

"Sexy twang, huh?" She was the most adorable thing when irritated. "You going to invite me in?" He didn't wait for an answer. He just took a step forward over the threshold and she took a step back.

"I don't guess I have to since you're already in."

Justin bit back a grin this time as he gazed at her. He couldn't help the urge. He wanted to let it split his mouth from ear to ear. She was full of fire, spit and vinegar, and had the sweetest, purest heart he'd ever known. All he wanted was for her to remember how good it had been and wanted to show her it could be that good again, even better long term and more often.

He nudged the door shut with the heel of his boot and looked around, trying to ignore the fidgeting she was doing beside him. Then he zeroed in on the suitcase sitting beside a small white table in the entryway. "Where're you goin'?"

"What? They didn't tell you that when you called the office? They'll give you my address but not my schedule?" She sighed. "Business trip. You really should have called, Justin. We could have arranged something when I got back."

"You mean like the last few times I've called and gotten the run around? You didn't leave me any other choice." He shook his head. He wasn't falling for that again. "Things have been different with you the last couple of months. You're pulling away and I don't understand why. We rarely talk for any length of time. You tell me about the places you've been and your work, but I want to know about you, how you're doin'. I'm tired of you pushing me away." And he sounded like a goddamn whiny little girl. God help him, but the woman was enough to drive a man insane.

"We talk, Justin."

He slanted a narrow gaze in her direction. "Not like we used to. We meet for the hottest damn sex on the planet, and sometimes we'll talk for a few days after, but it doesn't last. You pull away, put work in front of you as a shield until I have to practically beg you to meet me again. I want more than that, Ella. I've wanted more than that for a long fucking time."

"You don't like our weekends together?"

"You know I do. I love them." He started to tell her he loved more than their weekends, but she wasn't ready to hear it. "I want more though, and I'm here to work on it. Unless of course you tell me you don't want more than a few hot weekends of sex with me."

"Here to work on it?" Arms crossed over her chest, she cocked one hip out to the side. "You giving me an ultimatum, cowboy?"

She called him cowboy. That was a damn good sign. "Not at all."

"How are you planning to, as you say, work on it? I'm leaving. You going to camp out in my apartment until I get back?"

Her defiance and sassiness and smart mouth he could handle. It was her silence and her excuses he couldn't deal with. "Nope. And just for the record, I don't think you can do it."

She leveled a confused look at him. "Do what?"

"Tell me you don't want more from me than sex every few weekends."

11

"I can so," she scoffed with a tilt of her chin.

Justin gave no outward reaction, he just waited. Sometimes having a little brother paid off in ways one might never expect. Such as staring contests with the woman you want more than your next breath. He stared her down until she blinked. He grinned. "You'd be lying." Leaning down until his face was level with hers, he asked softly, "Are you going to start lying to me now, Ella?" Her gaze darted away and she started nibbling on her lower lip. He knew then he had her. He took a few steps until he was standing so close he could feel the heat coming off her body, see the pulse pounding in her neck. "Tell me I'm wrong. Tell me you don't want more, tell me you get everything you want and need from these little weekend meetings. Tell me..."

"Justin..."

"Tell me, Ella. Tell me and I'll go." Like hell. He'd driven ten hours from Dallas to Birmingham to get to her. No way was he leaving without her. He had a plan, and he was going to stick to it. He'd only leave if she meant it, and her eyes would tell him if her words were sincere and true.

He'd promised himself he wouldn't put his heart out there again since his ex had cheated on him. He swore he'd never allow himself to get so hooked on anyone, but Ella had wormed her way inside him with little more than a smile, and the early conversations they'd had during trivia nights in the downtown Birmingham bar where they'd met last year. Add in the daily emails, hours of instant messages, text messages and phone calls... Hooked didn't even begin to cover it.

She shook her head and pressed herself against him as he stood up straight again. She rubbed her face against his chest and sighed. "I can't."

For a moment, he stood stock still, but then wrapped his arms around her body and pulled her as close as he could. He brushed his lips against the top of her soft-as-silk hair before threading one hand into it. He tugged and she lifted her head. There were questions and even a few tears swimming in her eyes. He didn't want to see that, didn't want to be the cause of any pain, only the most intense pleasure.

He lowered his head, intent on a soft, small kiss, but was surprised when she threw her hands up to grip his hair and stood on tiptoe, crushing her mouth to his. Her tongue was between his lips and her fists were yanking at him before letting go and slipping to the buttons on his black button-down. He didn't make any move to stop her. If she wanted to undress him, he was more than willing to let her.

Once she had his shirt undone, he dropped his arms from around her and let her open it across his chest. She scraped her fingernails down his torso, just the way he liked, tender with a little bit of bite. She didn't stop there though. No, she kept going, right on to the button on his jeans, followed by the zipper going down at the insistence of her fingers. He watched her gain access to his body, felt the keen pleasure at her touch, wanted nothing more than to put her on the floor and rut with her until they were both exhausted, but he didn't. He gave her the freedom to do whatever she wanted, waited to see what she was after.

Ella pushed his jeans to his hips, letting his cock spring free before backing away and inching up her bright floral knee-length skirt. She kicked off her little sandals as she bared herself. All that separated him from being inside her was about three feet of distance and a pair of lime-green lace panties.

Once she'd backed herself against one of the entryway walls, he closed the three feet and reached for the lace.

13

"You wantin' somethin', Ella?" He'd give her the fucking moon if she asked for it.

She pushed her hips toward him and he snagged the crotch of her lace panties in his fist. She let out a little hiss and nodded her head. "You. Inside me."

He'd always loved that she would voice exactly what she wanted when it came to sex. That was just it though. Sex was the only area she wasn't shy about. It was such a turn on too. She liked him in control, he'd learned that early on, but she knew exactly what she wanted and needed in order to get aroused and get off. She was a confusing minx, and one he had loved figuring out. With the standoffish ways she'd been acting, though... It was time to change things up a bit. It was time to get into her mind, her soul, her heart. "Change of heart from a few minutes ago when I walked in the door. You couldn't wait to get rid of me."

She groaned in frustration. "Still want you gone, Justin. I have a plane to catch, but dammit you know I can't stop wanting you when you're around."

"That's what I'm counting on, baby, but I'm not going anywhere. Not again. Not without you." He fisted the lace in his palm and rubbed the back of his knuckles against her very smooth, very hot and very wet slit. She braced herself against the wall and spread her legs for him. "You're still such a good girl for me," he murmured. "Now why don't you tell me why you want me gone?"

"Won't...work. This... Us. Too needy..."

The breathlessness of her voice, the panting, the slickness coating his hand told of her need, but to hear her say it, to hear the words drove him on. "Yes, it will. Needy is very good, baby. You just have to let me in. You just have to trust me."

She hitched her skirt higher, and with her other hand, started working on the buttons of her own button-down. "No, no it can't. Lust. Hot. Need. Please, Justin."

"Lust is good. We can work with lust, I promise." Hell, he'd take all the lust she had to give and then some.

The first time they'd been alone together it was all he could do to get a breath in, get a word in because her mouth was constantly attached to his or to some other part of his body. Not that he was complaining. Then or now. He'd never been with a woman so full of fire and hunger. Insatiable didn't even come close to describing their encounter.

"Too much sex."

Justin nipped at her chin. "Never too much sex."

Ella nodded and pulled the sides of her shirt open, revealing the soft curve of her belly, the full curves of her breasts. Damn, they were still enough to drive him to his knees. She was a little smaller than the last time he'd seen her, but she still filled his hands and that's all he wanted, all he craved.

He pulled down one cup of her pink with lime-green lace-trim bra until he could get at her nipple, rock hard in the cool air of the room. Rasping his thumb over it, and then leaning in to scrape his two-day-old scruff over it, he was able to pull a moan from her.

"Please, Justin, please," she whimpered, at once pushing back into the wall and pushing herself into him.

He curled his tongue around her nipple and tugged it into his mouth as he pushed his hand upward, parting the lips of her sex with his knuckles. She sighed and ground her clit on him. Her hands were in his hair, on his shoulders, his arms. She was restless, unnerved, hungry and just the way he wanted her, just the way he planned to keep her. He wanted that moment of arousal, that one precious moment where nothing and no one else mattered but being kept on the edge.

That's where he needed her.

He pulled his hand away a little, enough that she protested with a high pitched "No". Looking up, he found her eyes were closed tight, her mouth slack, and he lifted his head, pressing his lips to hers, sinking his tongue inside and uttering a moan of his own when she threw her arms around him again and anchored herself to his body, fusing their mouths in a kiss as potent as poison. She could kill him with her kisses. She could render him weak and unable to form a thought when her tongue slid against his.

But he wouldn't let that happen. Not yet at least. He needed the control.

She sank lower, seeking more contact on her clit. She liked a solid pressure, and she liked to rock back and forth hard until she got the orgasm she was craving. He wasn't going to let her have it. He wanted to, but he couldn't afford to let her gain that upper hand.

"Nuh-uh, baby, not yet," he murmured against her lips. His cock ached to be inside her, be in her mouth, or hell, at this point just the touch of her fingers would do. He wanted it all as much as she did. He wanted the release that would flow through him and into her. But just as he was denying her, he was denying himself.

"Please, Justin," she pleaded. Her breathing picked up and her voice had those hungry and aroused panic tones again.

He let go of the crotch of her panties and dragged the tip of his fingers through her slit, teasing her clit between two of them, urging frantic whimpers from the back of her throat. She bucked against his touch.

"Yes. God yes, Justin... Right there... Oh..."

He slid the fingers away from her clit slowly and swallowed her cry of dismay. He pressed those same two fingers inside her, and then a third, fucking her in a delicious simulation of what he wanted to do with his cock.

Her hands clutched at his shoulder, and she bounced on his hand. "So close, Jus... I'm so close..."

"I know. Do you want it, El?"

"Oh God yes, please."

"How bad?"

"So bad. Don't. Stop." Desperation laced her voice.

Justin lifted his head and looked down at the woman against the wall, impaled on his fingers. Her hair was mussed and sticking out at odd angles. Her pink lipstick was smeared. Her cheeks were flushed, along with her neck. Her clothing was wrinkled beyond repair, unless she got out the iron. She was more beautiful than he remembered and he loved seeing her come undone like this, giving into the needs of her body.

Their weekends... She might think they were all about sex, but they weren't. He'd been falling for her for so long, and when she finally made a move, that rainy night outside the bar... It had taken months for her to give over to him, to give into the sexual attraction between them, but once she did and they walked through that hotel room door... Damn, he'd never been fucked like that.

Once he'd gotten her to orgasm for him that first time, to believe that he wanted it for her as much as she wanted it, to believe that he didn't care how wet she got or how wild and loud she got... She didn't seem to stop coming after that, and he only wanted more.

Hell, he'd been half in love with her by the time they fell asleep in the wee hours of the morning and by the time he got in his truck to head home to Texas, he still wanted her, still craved her.

All these months later, nothing had changed in the way he felt about her.

It had all started innocently enough with weekly trivia and beer in the downtown Birmingham bar. Justin eventually had given her his email address, and they'd chatted online late into the night when neither could sleep. Then there were the text messages, online trivia and word games, some flirting. Each connection with her drew him like a moth to a flame.

Every now and then, her naughty side would come out and it'd make him smile and ache in ways no other woman in recent memory had. Those months of getting to know her, of learning about her, of her opening up and letting him in while she rediscovered herself...that was worth every bit of effort he was willing to put into this. All he wanted was a chance to be more than her sometimes weekend lover. All he wanted was for her to let him in again.

Now, he had her in his arms and she was quivering, on the brink of coming for him. She still had her pretty green eyes tightly closed and her swollen-from-his-kisses bottom lip pulled once more between her teeth.

"Ella, baby," he whispered before licking at her lips. She moaned and nodded her head. "I want to take you back to Texas with me for a few days."

Her eyes flew open, and she stopped moving. "I can't," she protested immediately, albeit a bit breathlessly.

He didn't stop thrusting his fingers inside her, didn't stop staring at her. "You can."

She shook her head even as she started grinding on the invasion of the digits. She pinched at her own nipples, pulled and tugged, and then let go, and he was mesmerized by the gentle sway as they bounced. "Please let me come, Justin."

"Say you'll come to Texas with me and I'll let you." He wouldn't, but he was hoping she'd take the bait. He lowered his head and took a nipple between his teeth and gave it the same rough attention she'd given it with her fingers. She hissed her breath out between her teeth and groaned.

"Y-you know I can't."

Justin pulled his fingers from her soaked, hungry pussy and stepped back. He began stroking his cock as he watched her try to regain her senses. Her mouth opened and closed, but no sound or words came out. Her eyes were still wide, staring. He'd wait her out again.

They made a lewd picture. Horny and wanton, half undressed, facing off in her entryway.

"I can't believe you did that to me," she finally managed, though her gaze had dropped and was glued to the movement of his hand on his cock. He tried not to smile. Tried very hard. She loved his cock, he knew that. From the first moment she'd seen it, uncut and hard, she'd been fascinated, unable to take her eyes off it. The uncut part always caught women off guard. Some liked it, some didn't. Ella went after it like a starving woman.

And he was always hard when it came to her, whether he was thinking about her or within touching distance. "I'm not taking no for an answer."

"You can't force me to go with you."

He could, but... "No. You'll come willingly enough."

Her head shot up. "And you think that, why?"

"You want me and I want you. This is real, Ella. You know it, you feel it."

"Sex, Justin."

She didn't even believe her own words. He could see it in her eyes—hear it in the lack of conviction in her voice. "More than."

Her gaze searched his face then drifted down his body to his hand on his cock again. She licked her lips as he stroked the skin over the shaft. He wasn't sure she was even aware of it or that she moved her own hand up over her belly to her breast. She toyed with a nipple for a few seconds then stopped. She shook her head and looked him in the eye.

"I can't come to Texas, Justin. I'm on my way out to catch a flight for New Orleans."

"But you don't have to be there for your training classes for another couple of days, right? I'm guessing Tuesday or Wednesday." She started to say something but shut her mouth. Justin smiled. Caught. "You forgot you'd told me about that, didn't you? That you like to get to the location early to prepare yourself, to gauge the hotel's surroundings, observe its clients and traffic?"

She nodded. "But Justin..."

"You haven't given me one good reason, Ella. Not one. I want to take you home with me. I want to see you in my bed. I want to wake and see you snuggled so cute under my blankets." His voice dropped low and deep, the drawl slow and smooth, just the way he knew she liked it. "Here's the deal. Either give in and cancel or change your flight today, or..." He reached into his back pocket with his free hand and pulled out a piece of rope he'd coiled before knocking on her door and let it unwind in front of her face. "I'll have to tie you up and take my hand to your sweet ass until you agree."

"You wouldn't," she whispered.

He raised a brow and smiled, just a lazy stretching of his lips. "No?"

"Dammit, Justin." She stomped her foot. "This isn't how friends behave."

"Friends? That's what you think we are?" He stalked forward again and pressed her into the wall with his body. He let his cock rest against her belly and put both his hands on the wall beside her head. He leaned in and allowed the rope to dangle between her breasts. "We are so much more than friends, Ella. Your body knows that, even if your brain is unwilling to admit it."

She was silent for so long, just stood there between him and the wall, her breathing erratic, her fingers toying with the edges of his shirt, every so often brushing against his skin. The bright green rope alongside the pink of her bra and the spring colors of her clothes did dirty things to his mind. He loved the innocent, sweet outward appearance she presented, but when he stripped her to her bra and panties and even further to her nudity, she was more sex kitten than he'd ever imagined. She was his fantasy.

The rope turned her on. The thought of him spanking her until she gave in turned her on too. He didn't need her to tell him that. Not again, at least. They'd emailed at length about those naughty desires after their first time together. They'd explored them a little the next few times they met up. Being kinky in those swanky hotel rooms she'd gotten them into at no charge because she worked for the company was like a dirty little secret.

She knew he wasn't teasing about tying her up. She knew it was more than sex between them too. He'd made his feelings for her clear countless times over the last nine months they'd been seeing one another and every once in a while she'd slip up

21

and drop the walls around her heart, admitting she had feelings for him too. For some reason though, she'd put them on hold, her feelings and her relationship with him. He couldn't figure out why and that's what he needed to find out.

He was hoping that having her in Texas would give him some advantage over her, give him some way to bring out her vulnerability, break her defences down enough to figure out what in the hell spooked her so. He knew about her failed marriage, her divorce, but both were done and over with. At least, that's what he thought. Maybe feelings for her ex still lingered.

The groan that inadvertently slipped from his lips brought him out of his thoughts. He looked down to find that she was caressing the head of his cock with her thumb. Drive. Him. Insane.

One minute guarded and defiant. The next trying to get her way. "Naughty girl, Ella."

"Please, Justin. Just let me come once, please and I'll go with you." Her voice was a breathless whisper against his chest, her teeth nipping at his right nipple.

He tightened his lips and grunted. She played so damn dirty and he was so proud of her for it. "You'll go with me regardless of whether we screw once or half a dozen times before we get out the door. But, you're not in charge here." He brushed his lips against the edge of her hair at her temple and carefully stepped back again. It was harder than he thought. He wanted that touch so bad he could literally taste it on his tongue from her last kiss.

"You're impossible," she grumped.

He grinned. "That's what you said the first time you saw me naked and looked down."

"That's not what I mean." But she was fighting a grin too.

And she lost. From ear to ear, her lips split into a beautiful, toothy smile. That's what he wanted, that's what he'd come for. Her happiness. "So, are you going to make me tie you up and spank you into submission, or are you going to come willingly?"

She jerked her bra in place over her breast and started to button her shirt. "You're the one who deserves a spanking," she grumbled.

"If you're real nice, I might let you," he offered before he even knew what was going to come out.

Her gaze zoomed in on his, her mouth going slack. Heat flared in her green eyes, and she licked her lips. Damn. He was in trouble now. He winked.

She huffed and untwisted her panties then straightened her skirt. His cock grew another few degrees harder at the fleeting sight of her fingers against the bright lime lace of her underwear. "You're the worst sort of tease."

"I'm nothing of the kind. I mean everything I say to you."

"You would never let me spank you."

He tucked himself, painful as it was, back inside his jeans and reached for her. She didn't fight him and melted into his body as he fisted his hand in her disheveled hair and brushed his lips against hers. "Do you really want to? Do you really want me to let you spank me?"

"I might," she murmured.

He didn't have the heart to deny her anything. "I'll let you, but..."

She pushed at him but his hold remained firm. "See, I knew you wouldn't let me."

"But," he started again. "Only after you let me remind you what it's like between us."

Her gaze met his, open and completely defenseless. "I'm scared, Justin."

"I know. I wish you'd let me help."

They stayed that way, him holding her for long moments before her arms wrapped around his back and she laid her cheek against his chest. She was strong, beautiful and vulnerable. He wanted to care for her, take care *of* her, wipe the shadows from her eyes.

"I have to be in New Orleans on Wednesday."

Inwardly, Justin was fist pumping. Outwardly, he was just holding her close. "You will be."

"I can't promise anything beyond that."

"I know, but I can."

"Justin..."

He shook his head and squeezed her tight. He spoke into her hair. "Call and take care of your flight. I'll make sure you get to Louisiana when you need to be there."

"Why are you doing this?" she sighed.

"You know why. I'm not going to spell it out for you. Not yet at least. You're just going to have to accept that you need me to show you more than you need the words."

"I like words," she said softly, rubbing her cheek against his nipple.

It was his turn to hiss a breath out between his teeth. "You like filthy, naughty words, but in the case of other kinds of words, you need action. Action you'll believe." She turned and bit his nipple again, though harder this time, and a yelp flew from his lips. "Dammit, woman."

Ella giggled and the sound slid through him like honey. She pushed out of his arms and took her purse off the table by the door. "You better hope they can change it instead of

24

canceling it or I will be taking it out of your hide." Pulling her airline ticket from inside, followed by her cell phone, she looked over at him and licked her lips. His knees threatened to buckle at the look in her eyes. She wouldn't say it out loud, the words the look on her face conveyed. Not yet anyway. But he was hoping by the time she left for New Orleans, she will have uttered those three little words.

"You can put the rope away. I'll come with you."

Justin inclined his head in acknowledgement and coiled the soft nylon around his hand before slipping it into his back pocket again. "For now. I'll put it away for now."

Chapter Two

Ella stood on the sidewalk holding her carry-on as Justin loaded her suitcase and laptop bag into the backseat of the black extended cab truck. It gleamed in the early afternoon sunshine. From what she could see, it had a dark gray fabric interior with black piping. It fit him. It wasn't what he'd been driving all these months, but since she hadn't seen him for the last two or three...

"Okay. Hand me the bag you're holding." She held it out to him, and he stowed it with her others. "Anything else?" He asked, looking around.

"Nope. Just me."

"Come on then. You're the most important thing." He gestured for her, and she stepped down and met him at the passenger door. He blocked the opening with his body. "Take your panties off."

Her eyes widened then narrowed as her brow furrowed. "What? Justin, I can't do that."

"You've been full of more can'ts today... Why not?"

"Not out here in the parking lot. You should have said something back in the apartment."

"Would you have done it then?"

She hesitated. Part of her said yes, she would have. Another part of her said no, she wouldn't. A third part of her didn't want anything to do with the argument. "I can't do it out here," she protested again. "What if my neighbors see?"

"No one can see you at this angle. They can only see your feet, and if you're quick about it..." He shrugged. "You're not getting in my truck until those panties are off."

"When did you get so bossy?" she grumbled, even as she reached under her skirt and started to slide her panties over her hips and thighs. Nervously, she glanced around as she quickly shimmied them down her legs.

"I've always been bossy. And when I want somethin', I want it." He knelt before she could move and took hold of the green lace at her feet.

She lifted one foot, then the other. When he stood again, he grinned, brought the panties to his nose and sniffed. The dreamy look was wonderful and the waggling of his eyebrows as he looked her over with lascivious intent made her giggle. She might think this was a very bad idea, going all the way to Texas with him, letting him take her back to his home, his bed, his territory, but she would bet every penny she had that he was going to make every bit of it worth her while and then some.

He moved out of her way, and she took a couple of cautious steps forward before climbing up into the seat. He gave her a little lift with his hands around her waist and helped her settle. "Don't think I don't know what you're up to with that little panties game."

His fingers deftly unbuttoned the top two buttons of her shirt and left it gaping open enough that anyone looking in the window, either from the side or from the front would be able to see the edges of her bra and the cleft between her breasts. She should be upset and angry with him, and she sort of was, but not enough to put up a fuss. She wanted him far too much and he'd see right through her. All fight left her the second she'd agreed to spend the next couple of days with him.

She'd spent more than half a dozen weekends with him having the best sex of her life and knew what she was getting into. She'd been friends with him, lovers with him. She trusted him. And that he came for her?

It couldn't have been an easy decision for him. She'd learned as much about him as he'd learned about her over the months of correspondence. He didn't chase after women. He'd told her that more than once. He simply let them go when they wanted to leave, despite his comment a few minutes ago about when he wanted something. That didn't apply to women. Not usually.

The thing was, since their first time together, she never wanted to leave him.

"What do you mean you know what I'm up to?"

Ella looked at him. He was standing between her and freedom. His hair was longer and a bit shaggier than before. His eyes were still the same mercurial shade of green framed by dark brows and lashes. His mouth was still sinfully full, and when he smiled, she was worthless for anything else. He was a tall, very good-looking twenty-nine year old man and it never once occurred to her that she didn't deserve him, that she was too old or that he was too young, that she was too heavy or that he was too irresistible. He wanted her, and she wanted him.

If her heart had really been in it, before, in the apartment or even now, sitting in his truck, she could say no. She could put her foot down and tell him to go. They both knew he would if he believed she wanted him to. They both knew she wouldn't be able to convince him with words, anymore than he could convince her with them, when her body and her eyes said something very different than go away.

"You're trying to strip away my defenses."

"Your panties are a defense?"

Okay, well, when he put it that way, it sounded kind of dumb because how much of an actual defense was a pair of lace panties? "You know what I mean."

"No."

"No?"

"That isn't what I'm going for here, Ella. Accessible, yes. Flashable, yes. Strong and sexy, yes. But defenseless? No."

He leaned forward and kissed her on the nose, a sweet little peck that was so out of character for the man he'd been today. The contrast made her smile. "Accessible, huh?"

"Yep. And flashable."

"Flashable isn't even a word."

"Doesn't mean it isn't an idea." He shut the door, and her gaze tracked him as he walked around the front end of the truck to the driver's side.

He climbed up and reached across the center console to grip her thigh over her skirt. She watched as his fingers pulled the fabric up, inch by inch. She kept her legs tightly closed and glanced over at him. He only smiled and tugged on her left leg. His strength versus hers...

The second she relaxed against his touch, his hand was gone. "What? Why?"

"I just wanted to see how long you'd resist. I'm not going to force you to give in." He smiled, slow and wicked. "I don't have to force you to give in."

He was right, damn him. He hadn't forced her when they were upstairs. She put up token resistance, but the second she laid eyes on him standing at her front door, her insides had melted. The previous times she'd been with him had been the most eye-opening sexual experiences of her life. Eye-openingly emotional too. She still wasn't sure if that was a good thing or a bad thing. Emotions were messy and hard and hurt.

"How long of a drive is it?" she asked as he cranked the truck and put it in reverse.

"Little over ten hours."

Ella looked at the clock on the dash. "But, that means you'd have driven most of the night to get here." It was only just after one in the afternoon.

"Yes."

"Why?"

"'Cause I wanted to get here as soon as I could. Nothin' but truckers on the road at three in the morning. Damn good thing I did or I'd have missed you."

Yes, he would have. She'd been headed out the door when he knocked. He was the last person she expected to see, but she wouldn't deny how happy it made her to find him there, smiling at her in that lop-sided-tilt-of-the-lips way that she saw in her mind's eye and in her dreams.

It was time to change the subject. "When did you get the truck?" It was brand new or at least no more than a year old. The shiny red wood of the dash, the plush fabric of the seats gave the interior a feeling of warmth, and even though the center console separated her from him, he was close enough to touch and vice versa.

"Parents and brother went in with me for the truck for my birthday, plus I manage the bar now."

Silly as it was, that was always one of her favorite things about him. He was a bartender. It gave him an air of wildness.

And he was bartender in a Texas bar in a little Texas town. Something about that turned her on. He was a cowboy at heart, running cattle for his family's ranch, but he'd put himself through college bartending, and right after they'd started seeing one another, he'd put in for training to become a volunteer firefighter.

He was so full of life and energy. She loved that and being around him made her feel full of life and energy and happy. Yet, she was fighting it with every fiber of her being.

"It's beautiful."

"Yeah. It was an awesome gift. I love it." He waggled his eyebrows at her and then winked. "Wait until you see the bed in the back."

So naughty. "Just make sure to put a few blankets down for some padding."

"Already ahead of you there, baby."

And...they needed to turn the conversation back to safe ground. "How's the firefighting going?"

"Luckily, we haven't had any to put out in a couple of months."

"You still like it?"

"I do. I love it. Between the bar and the fire department, plus helping out the folks on the ranch from time to time, I stay pretty busy."

Never too busy for her though. He didn't say it, but the words hung in the air just the same. "Not enough time to go chasing the girls, huh?" As if he would. She knew he was loyal, devoted to whatever woman he was seeing at any one time, and for the last months, it had been her. Trust in him was something she'd never questioned.

He shook his head. "You know me better than that."

Yes, she did. "You chased me." So much for safe topics.

"Yep. I probably know you better than I've ever known anyone."

"That makes it different?"

"Of course it does. You didn't expect me to chase you. You didn't expect me to show up. Ever."

He had her there. "Well, aren't you just full of surprises?"

"More than you'll ever know, baby."

Ella decided that comment was best left alone. She was curious about the things he had up his sleeve, but she was smart enough to know he was stubborn enough not to reveal anything to her. She turned her head to the side and propped her chin on her hand, watching the countryside pass by.

Her apartment was outside the city limits of Birmingham and because she traveled a lot for work, it didn't make sense to her to pay the higher prices for convenience. Besides, she liked that it was a lot quieter out where she was, less hectic but close to the interstate, grocery stores and a park with walking trails. It was suburbia, and she was a suburbanite without the husband, kids and pets.

"Do you need me to stop anywhere before we get up on the highway?"

Justin's question tugged her attention back to him "No. I ate just before you showed up. I'm good for a while."

He smiled at her. "Okay."

She tried not to stare at him, and it took a few seconds before she was able to tear her gaze away. Looking out the window again, she contemplated him and what was happening, what had been happening over the past months. Giving into the attraction between them the day her divorce papers arrived had likely not been the brightest idea. Getting involved with him beyond that one night hadn't been part of her stay-uninvolved-for-at-least-a-year plan, either.

If she believed in fate, she'd swear it and Justin had begun conspiring the first night he walked into the bar. How else did one explain him showing up on trivia night, on the one night of the week she went out with friends? How else did one explain him showing up alone and just as there happened to be someone in her group who had canceled? And for three months, every week, he arrived at the bar, took a seat next to her and worked his way under her skin. That she'd filed for divorce from her husband the day she and Justin met wasn't lost on her.

Fate.

If she believed in it.

"You're awful quiet over there. You okay? Having second thoughts?"

"I'm good and no, not having second thoughts."

"Having third and fourth thoughts, then?"

Ella glanced at him and smiled. "No."

He smiled back. "Okay."

"Would it matter if I were having second or third thoughts?" She knew the answer.

"Prolly not."

He turned the radio on, a local country station, and he started tapping his fingers on the steering wheel to the Sugarland song that came on. She didn't know the name of it or the words, but the voice of Jennifer Nettles was unmistakable.

"It's pretty much a straight shot on I-20 West until we get closer to Dallas."

"So you mean it's a pretty boring drive until we get closer to Dallas."

"Not at all. I have you to keep me company this time and you have me. I'm much better than a boring flight to New Orleans."

She had no doubt about that. He would make the trip interesting if nothing else, but then there was a whole lot of something else. Lust simmered between them at all times, but there were other things, important things too. Questions that needed answers floated invisibly in the air. Communicating had never really been a problem for them, at least not in the short-novel-sized letters they would email to one another. They'd been pretty good at talking on the phone too from time to time, whiling away the hours. They'd had their own inside jokes from the bar, but things changed once she was well and truly divorced.

That night was crystal clear in her mind.

"Look who I found wandering around outside in the rain."

Ella had been a little down that day. Her boss offered her a new position, one that would have her traveling all over, training front desk staff at new hotel properties and her marriage was gone, her divorce final, and loneliness had begun to set in. Then Justin walked in behind one of her friends who was notoriously late to everything. Ella knew right then if she said anything, did anything, that things would be different between them.

"I heard about your divorce. I'm sorry."

His words had said he was sorry, and she didn't doubt he meant them, but the look in his eyes, sincerity mixed with lust, did her in. She'd thought about him, fantasized about him often enough.

The night went on the way it usually did. For a couple of hours they all had drinks, bad-for-you bar food and played trivia games. She lost. Her mind was not on anything other than sex with Justin. He'd never said anything untoward, never even hinted at being interested in becoming more than friends until that night.

It was still raining when the bar closed and everyone had gone home. Only she and Justin were left standing outside. She wasn't sure who was more reluctant to leave, him or her. He offered to walk her to her car in the garage around the corner, and she offered to take him to the hotel across the street until morning.

Before he could answer, she'd stood on tiptoe and kissed him. She'd meant it to be nothing more than a small, almost chaste kiss, but the minute she touched his mouth with hers, she changed. It was instantaneous. Who'd ever heard of a kiss changing someone? She hadn't and she'd never experienced it. Until then. And if a kiss changed her inside, sex changed her everything, in every way.

And still, she had no idea why they'd ever really hit it off. Trivia nights had been fun. Sex was great. But he was right. It was more than sex. She liked to think it wasn't more, but she knew better. By saying it was just sex was the only way she knew to protect herself.

They had nothing in common really. He was single and carefree. She was divorced and a stick in the mud. He was taking a summer off and having a good time with friends. She was staid and solid and kept to herself when she wasn't traveling. He was laid back. She was a bit uptight. He liked country, and she liked rock and roll.

Ella smiled to herself and slid a glance in his direction. They both did like Elvis though and wished they hadn't been too young to see him before he'd died. Well, she'd been too young. Justin hadn't even been born yet. She tried not to groan at that realization.

Little by little, they forged a connection that had her staying up late at night talking to him long after she should have been asleep. "When did it change between us?" she asked suddenly. Would his answer be the same as hers?

"When did what change between us?"

She shifted in her seat, putting her back to the door and pulling a leg up, forgetting for a minute that she wasn't wearing any panties. She ended up flashing him with a peek up her skirt before adjusting it. "When did we become more than friends?"

"Do that again." He nodded his head in the direction of her lower body.

"No, you perv." She laughed. "Answer my question."

He shifted his gaze to her for a second, then back to the road, then back to her. "Flash me again and I will."

She thought to refuse him, but the thought ended quickly enough. He was more stubborn than she was. She lifted the end of her skirt, flashing her pussy at him for no more than the length of a quick breath, then dropped the skirt back to her lap. She should have been embarrassed by it, but she couldn't be, wouldn't be. She wanted him too much.

"Your turn."

"Can't flash you while I'm driving, baby, but you could always lean over here and..."

"Dirty man. Answer my question." There was no heat in her words, at least not the angry kind of heat. And there was a smile on her face as she'd said them.

"From the start, I never thought of you as just a friend. Maybe I should have, but I didn't. I wanted more than that right away."

"So it was just that easy for you?" Why was she so surprised? Her ex really wasn't a good example of the typical man.

His turn to be surprised. "Wasn't it for you?"

She was grown up enough to admit it, even if she didn't want to. "It was."

"Then what's the problem?"

He sounded sincerely concerned, and she couldn't blame him. It probably seemed that she was trying to borrow trouble where there was none. "I was married when we met, Justin," she said softly. She'd learned how very far from perfect she was, despite how many years she'd told herself that she was, that her husband was, that her marriage was. Perfect was nothing more than a wish, a dream and an illusion in the face of reality. And reality sucked sometimes.

"You were separated and had filed for divorce. People have feelings for married people all the time. Not saying that makes it right or wrong, just that it happens. I didn't act on my feelings. Having them isn't a crime."

Didn't stop her either apparently. "I know you're right."

"It was crazy, yeah?" He glanced at her then back out the windshield and folded his hands over the steering wheel. "If someone had told me I would meet and fall for a woman so damn hard from the word go, I'd have told them they were full of horseshit. I just don't, didn't trust women anymore. I'd just come out of a relationship. Come up here to Birmingham to spend some time with my buddies. I had planned on it to be for a few months, but then I was asked to fill in at the bar one of them worked in until someone permanent could be hired. I never expected to walk into another bar and be invited to sit at a table with, well anyone, and then there was you sitting in the corner."

"I was just a woman nursin' a beer and really not wanting to be there, so I'm not sure what you saw in me." She wasn't fishing for compliments. She really didn't know. She'd been sad and sullen and feeling like a complete and utter failure in the marriage department. Just because she had needs—or deviances as her ex put it—didn't mean she couldn't have tried harder.

But how do you tell your husband sex with him bores you? That was far from being the only thing wrong in her marriage, but it was definitely a contributing factor, especially when he wouldn't do anything or try anything or even consider anything beyond missionary and darkness.

"You smiled."

She focused on him. "What?"

"You smiled. The woman sitting next to you that first night leaned over and whispered something that made you smile. It was beautiful and I was hooked."

"Oh please, Justin. That only happens in books and movies. It doesn't even happen on television and it sure doesn't happen in the real world."

"I didn't think so either, but I was a changed man that night. It's why I kept coming back each week, you know."

He blushed at his own words and that along with his confession only served to endear him more to her. "No, I didn't know."

His answer was to smile and nod his head.

"Regrets?"

"Nope. Not a one. I wouldn't change anything that happened or the way it happened for anything. You?"

Her cell phone rang as he asked, and she was thankful for the distraction. He must have seen the relief on her face because he laughed. She stuck her tongue out at him and answered it. "Hello?"

"Ella? I just called the property in New Orleans and found out you'd changed your reservations to arrive on Wednesday. Is everything all right? Are you all right?"

It was her boss, Barb, and for some reason, likely the man seated behind the wheel, Ella hadn't thought to call the poor woman and let her know about the changes. She wouldn't have given Barb any specific details about her change of plans, but she should have called at least. "Yes, everything is fine. Something personal came up at the last minute."

"Oh," came the relieved tone of voice on the other end. "Do we need to reschedule the class? Do you need a few more days off?"

"No, I'll be there. I just needed to take care of some other things instead of going early."

Justin slid a glance in her direction and smirked at her. She smirked back. How else did one explain to their boss that they were headed off to have very naughty sex instead of showing up for work early? It's not as if she was lying when she said some other things had come up and she needed to take care of them. He'd come up and she needed to take care of him.

Although, he needed to take care of her too. She still hadn't forgiven him for leaving her as hungry as he had a little bit ago.

"That's good," Barb was saying. "Then I'll just send this paperwork on to the hotel anyway and ask them to hold it for you."

"Thanks, Barb. I appreciate it."

"And you're sure you're all right? You know you can come to me about anything. I hope we've established that kind of rapport."

Ella smiled at the concern and reminder of friendship. She usually wasn't one who had last-minute things come up. She usually wasn't one who had to change or wanted to change her work or travel schedule. She was one who liked the routine and the structure that she'd set up in her personal life over the last six months or so and understood how her sudden change would cause worry. "Yes, I'm sure. I'm sorry. I know I should have called you. I just didn't have a chance."

"Well, so long as you're all right. I'll talk to you in a couple of days."

"Okay." Ella hung up and looked over at the man driving, the one she'd had to step outside her normal routine for. "I hope you're happy."

"For the moment, yep."

"For the moment?"

"I'll be even happier when I get you in bed, naked and under me."

Of all the answers she thought he might give, for some odd reason, that wasn't what she'd expected and she felt heat creep up her neck and fill her face. She also felt a smile stretch her lips. She wanted nothing more than to be naked with him, and she didn't care about their positions.

He gave her a matching smile. "You're thinking about it too, huh?"

"Yep." No use in denying it. "We could stop in Shreveport or something. My hotel has a new property there. We could—"

"No, we couldn't. I want you in my house, in my bed. I'm not fuckin' you until then."

Ella slowly shifted her legs and lifted her skirt. "But Dallas is such a long way away," she teased, followed by a yelp when he snagged her ankle and tugged her leg out straight across the console.

"Dallas is a very long way, but I intend to play with you some until we get there."

She pulled against his hold but he wouldn't let up. "Meanie."

"Don't even try that shit. You know I'm gonna keep my word. I'll fuck you as soon as we get to my place and I can get you inside."

"I don't mean that. You're planning on teasing me the whole way. Just like you did in my apartment. You're going to tease me then leaving me hanging on the edge."

"I didn't say that, but now that you mention it..." He winked and let his finger caress the side of her ankle, up the side of her calf and farther up to her knee.

She did her best not to moan, but when his hand reached higher to her thigh, she couldn't help it. The man had that magic touch. She remembered thinking about the old Heart song, "Magic Man", when she'd driven away from him after that first night. He'd made her body do things, feel things no man ever had.

And since she'd seen him standing outside her door this afternoon, all she could think about was him getting his hands on her and his cock inside her. Everything about him caused everything inside her to zing to life. She wanted him and quite possibly more now than she had before.

She moved in the seat one more time and stretched her other leg out to rest alongside the one he already had. She leaned back against the door and tilted her head to lay it on the headrest. Slowly, he stroked her legs. He didn't reach under her skirt, simply stroked to the hem and then down again to her ankle.

His touch was soothing and comforting. He still had the radio on, though turned down since her phone call and her eyes grew heavy, sleepy. She'd never been a good passenger on road trips, always falling asleep within a few miles down the road.

She tried to keep her eyes open, her gaze on him, but his fingers were lulling her to sleep and she gave up trying to fight it.

Chapter Three

"Justin, please."

He loved reducing her to begging him for release. With her thighs draped over his shoulders and her muscles quivering, she was all but putty in his hands. He blew warm breath against her sex and squeezed her bottom in his hands.

She'd slept all the way through to Shreveport, even through him stopping for gas. The rest stop was fairly deserted and as soon as he had her creaming on his tongue, he'd set them to rights again and get back on the road.

She lifted up, or tried to lift her upper body, but the ropes tying her to the hooks in the bed of the truck only gave her so much pull. Her heels dug into his shoulder blades in an attempt to leverage herself closer to his mouth.

"Damn you, Jus... Please..." Breathless from arousal and winded from exertion as she tried to reach her goal, she sighed in frustration and relaxed.

Justin licked at her clit, slowly with the tip of his tongue, savoring the feel of her, the taste of her. A moan escaped her lips and the tremors in her thighs picked up again.

Lifting his gaze, he looked up her body. Her shirt was still on, though unbuttoned again, and he could see the swells of her breasts over the cups of her bra. The late afternoon sun was half hidden behind the trees and cast just enough light down on the bed that rays and shadows melded together across her stomach.

He dipped his head and slid his tongue inside her, pulling wetness out, enough for him to coat her lower lips and get her clit all silky and slippery. Her hands fisted, and she tugged against the ropes, helpless. He wanted control, and it hadn't taken much for him to steal it from her.

Long, slow kisses as he'd walked her toward the back of the truck, left her clinging to his neck. He'd pulled the tailgate down and maneuvered her to a sitting position on it. She spread her legs willingly to allow him between them.

Years of working his parents' ranch left him very, very good with rope, and he'd had her wrists tugged down from the back of his neck and bound before she'd ever known what happened. Her eyes hazy with lust and need, she'd only given token protest to being laid back and secured among the old blankets and soft quilts he'd brought along on the trip for this specific purpose.

He wanted her helpless and hungry. He wanted her control stripped and her desires to shine. He wanted what she'd given to him before. He wanted it back. He wanted *her* back, and he wasn't above using her want of him to get it.

She wiggled in his hands and he removed one from her ass cheeks to pop the flat of his fingers against her pussy. A surprise yelp followed by a low moan made him do it again. The moan was louder that time. He grinned. His little kitten still liked it.

He leaned in and tasted the newly plumped pussy and she writhed, sensitive to even the barest of touches, of licks, of breaths.

Tugging again on the ropes that held her arms stretched above her head, she whined a protest at his teasing.

"Had enough, pet?"

She growled. "Had enough before you started. Please just let me come already."

"Now where would the fun be in that?" As he spoke, his breath fanned the wet and open sex in front of him. Her scent wafted toward his nose and goosebumps coated her skin.

"You're mean and cruel and evil and I just don't like you," she protested while at the same time digging her heels into his shoulder blades again, pulling herself up toward his lips.

He nipped her clit with the edges of his teeth and just caught sight of a trickle of wetness leaking from her. If he'd blinked, he'd have missed it. He'd never seen anything sexier and licked at the droplet, taking it on his tongue before it could slide out of sight. He moved her legs from his shoulders and crawled up her body, sliding his tongue in her mouth, sharing her taste.

She whimpered into his kiss and wrapped her legs around his hips much as she had when he'd seated her on the tailgate. Cradling her head in his hands, lingering over the kiss that stole his breath, he ground his jeans-covered cock against her, the denim rubbing at her clit.

She tore her mouth away, and he looked at her with hooded eyes. She was riding him from below as much as he was riding her from above. Her gasps and gulps of air, her small whimpers and the trembling of her entire body drove him crazy.

Fucking her while he was still fully dressed and buttoned up was the best and worst of ideas. He wanted inside her so bad he could almost feel her heat close in around him. He was harder than a jackhammer and he rocked his hardness into her until she was wrapping her fingers around the ropes and holding on tight.

Justin lowered his mouth to her ear and fisted his hands in her hair. "Come, Ella. Come for me."

She nodded, and her mouth opened on a wordless, soundless cry... Then she wailed it out, bucking under him, bound in his ropes, giving herself up to him and to the teasing pleasure he'd induced.

He dropped his lips to her heaving chest, licked at the dark valley between her breasts, tasting the salt of her skin until she calmed beneath him. Her heartbeat was strong and thunderous, and when he looked up, he saw the tilt of her lips upward in a sated smile. Her eyes were closed, her fingers slack.

"Ella?" he whispered.

"Hmm?"

She still didn't open her eyes and her lips were still smiling. She was more beautiful than anything or anyone he'd ever seen.

"I think I... "

"Yeah?" came her breathy whisper.

"I think I need to change my jeans."

Her eyes flew open, and her mouth formed a tight, little O before she started giggling. He tugged on her hair, and though she winced slightly, she didn't stop laughing.

"And you find this funny, why?" Not that he was upset with her.

"You were so intent on being in control of me, and when I came *you* lost control."

She was right. "Yep. Teach me to use your pretty mouth before I start teasing and playing with you." He kissed the tip of her nose and sat, straddling her body just under the breasts and went to work on untying her arms.

Next thing he knew, she'd leaned forward and her mouth was fastened to his wet crotch. He tried not to groan but did it anyway. Before he could move away, she grabbed hold of his ass with one hand and was working the button and zipper of his jeans down with the other.

"What in the hell do you think you're doing?" There was no heat in his voice, only a croak of sound as she fastened her lips to his come-coated dick.

"Cleaning," she murmured in between licks.

"Shit." He grabbed at her hair again and held her against him as she cleaned. They would need to get going soon, but he wasn't ready to let her mouth leave him just yet. He might not have been hard anymore, but the pleasure zinging through him...

Their gazes clashed when she looked up and he looked down. She licked her lips and he sat back on his haunches, stealing her tongue into his mouth, tasting himself on her the same as he'd shared her taste when he'd kissed her before.

"Justin," she said softly when he pulled back.

"Yeah, baby."

"I think you're still gonna have to change your jeans."

She'd said it so seriously, so matter-of-factly that he laughed and wondered what in the hell he'd gotten himself into with her.

"We ever gonna talk about it?"

Ella turned her head toward him. "Talk about what?" She feigned innocence though she knew without having to be told what exactly it was that Justin wanted to talk about.

"You know what."

"I don't really want to." She sighed and took the lifeline he offered when he reached for her hand.

He slid his fingers between hers and squeezed lightly. It wasn't the first time he'd asked, but in emails and texts and instant messages, she could avoid the subject better and easier than she could with him seated a foot away.

"I know you don't want to and I don't want to push it. Part of me thinks you'll tell me when you're ready, but the other part of me thinks that unless I prod you and make you tell me, that you never will."

He was right about that. "That's the thing. I don't know when I'll be ready." And she didn't. She might never be and that just wasn't acceptable if she was going to ever move forward and have another relationship. Whether it was with Justin or not, she would have to get to a place where she could be and would be ready to open up and talk about her marriage.

"We weren't suited, you know? He and I. We just weren't compatible in..." Damn she sounded as if it were more a business arrangement or friendship than a marriage. "I had this idea of what being married would be, of what a relationship between a husband and wife should be and the reality didn't live up to it."

"How so?"

"I used to think that a marriage was two people who wanted to be with one another, two people who couldn't imagine life apart. I didn't really feel that with him, and I don't think he ever felt it with me either. I think it was more or less that neither of us wanted to be alone. It's not that I expected roses and wine and to be attached at the hip all day and night. I just wanted his attention, his affection, sex. I wanted someone to talk with, share life with, and after giving in, in nearly every area of his interest and getting nothing in return..." She shrugged and tried to pull her hand from his, to put some distance between them, but Justin wouldn't let go. She was open and feeling exposed and she hated it. Sexually exposed she could handle. Emotionally, not so much.

"You deserved better. You still do, baby."

"So did he. It just wasn't working out and I didn't want to hurt him more than I had already by pushing him away, by not being able to accept that he wasn't going to change or be able to let me in the way I needed him to. Even though I understood his reasons for keeping everything so bottled up, even though I was doing exactly what he tried to protect himself against, I needed more from him. I didn't want a fairy tale, but I wanted more than I was getting. I was starving for affection, for closeness, for any kind of connection, and he wasn't capable of giving it."

She thought back to all those conversations, to the look in his eyes, to the disappointment, to the anger, to the relief. He knew she hadn't been happy for a long time because she'd told him on more than one occasion. He didn't ask her to stay to try and fix things. He didn't promise he'd try to change. She was emotionally and sexually needy and she knew it, and staying with him wasn't going to help her fulfill those needs.

"I'm sorry, Ella."

"No need for you to be sorry, Justin, but thank you just the same."

"Do you regret it?"

Did she? "No. My mom always said that when it was time, I'd know. She'd realized even before I did how unhappy I was. I wasn't fair to him. I should have let him go long before. I wasted eight years of his life and mine. I knew before we ever walked down the aisle that I shouldn't marry him, that something wasn't clicking, but I did it anyway."

She didn't need or want to make excuses, drum up reasons why or what if. What was done was done. She couldn't undo it, she couldn't take it back, and even if she could, she wouldn't. "I should have walked away long before I did."

"Why didn't you?"

Why indeed. "Fear. I was scared no one else would ever want me. Strange to think that when I don't know that he ever wanted me to begin with. I just don't know. We were great as friends, bad as lovers."

Justin nodded. "I think a good marriage takes both."

She agreed with him on that.

"Do you still see him, talk to him?"

Ella smiled into the darkness outside the dim truck cabin. There was an odd intimacy surrounding them. There were cars and trucks with lights on, passing them on the road, but it was almost as though she and Justin were the only two people in the world. "Yes. We actually do still talk, more so than we did when we were married. He moved back home to Georgia, and oddly enough, I travel near there on occasion. We've met for lunch and dinner and talked about the things that made us friends but not lovers."

"Still no regrets?" he asked again.

She turned toward him. She couldn't tell what he was thinking or feeling. Since her separation and then her divorce, she'd vowed that no matter what, she'd be honest from then on. Whether it was about how she felt or didn't feel, what she wanted or didn't want, what was or wasn't working for her, she'd be honest. She wouldn't try to talk herself into someone else's truths or beliefs or feelings of what was best.

Just like with Justin. If she hadn't wanted to be with him, she wouldn't be riding in the truck, getting closer to Dallas and his home, his bed, with every second that ticked by. "No."

It was a few minutes before he spoke. "I have regrets," he said softly.

Her eyes widened as she stared at him. He had regrets? About them? She tried to pull her hand from his grip again, but he wouldn't let go. Was he having second thoughts about this? Maybe she should have put up a bigger fuss, pushed him harder about why he wanted her, why he'd come to see her and made the proposition he had. The only way she was going to find out what his regret was, was to ask. That was another form of honesty, asking the hard questions even if you were afraid to hear the answers. "What do you regret?"

"Not coming to get you sooner."

He said it so quietly that she almost didn't hear it, but for emphasis, he lifted her hand and stretched her over a bit so he could kiss it. Her heart stuttered to a near stop at his words, at the relief she felt. "Why didn't you?"

"Work is the easy answer. I knew you were busy and I couldn't get away at the time. It gave me an excuse to give you space in the hopes you'd come to me, that you'd let me in again, that you'd start talking to me, sharing with me again. You never did. I didn't understand why you kept pushing me away and the only way to find out was to put myself in front of you and force you to talk to me, to react to me. So, the first chance I got, I took it."

"Trickster."

"Whatever I had to or have to do to get you to open up again, baby, I'm ready, willing and able to do."

"I wish I were as confident about us as you." What if she could never have a serious relationship with anyone? What if it was more than the lack of affection and attention and sex? What if there was something wrong with her? She hadn't come from the most stable of homes.

Her father had an affair when he'd been married to her mother, and when he left her, he married the woman he'd been seeing, and to this day they were still married, happily. Her father hadn't been happy, not for many years before he'd left. Her stepmother was the exact opposite of her real mother, and those differences were overwhelmingly obvious. "I don't know, Justin."

"I don't *know* know either, baby, not for certain, but by your own admission there were doubts in your head before you got married and throughout you felt something wasn't right."

"I wanted more." And she had. She wanted more attention, more affection, more sex, more of everything. She'd turned into a homebody when what she'd really wanted was to go out and do things, be with people, but her husband wanted to sit and watch ball games and television shows. At first they'd sat on the couch together, but then he bought a recliner, and that small bit of togetherness, that little bit of intimacy was gone. Her marriage hadn't given her what she'd hoped for and she'd turned to going out with friends from work. He'd never seemed to mind. He did his thing and she did hers. They simply paid the bills together and shared a roof.

"I know you did. Some things just aren't meant to be, Ella."

"We might not be," she said solemnly, giving voice to one of her very real fears.

"True, but I'm inclined to believe we are." He slid her a wink and a waggle of his eyebrows in an effort to pull a smile from her. It worked.

"And why is that?"

"Many, many reasons."

His voice had dropped to that deep, seductive Texas twang she loved so much. It usually wasn't so pronounced, but there were moments where it took over and it was all she could do not to melt into a puddle. "Such as?"

"Well, there's the taste of you on my tongue. One just doesn't get over that."

Ella rolled her eyes in his direction and huffed. "Oh, I'm sure one does and can if one tries. What else have you got?"

"The taste of me on your tongue. One just doesn't get over that either."

She'd have laughed if he hadn't sounded so serious. She knew he was teasing her, trying to bring her out again, make her smile and believe in him, even if she didn't believe in them yet. "Arrogant ass. There's more, right? Something more substantial maybe?"

"Of course there is. You talk to me and I talk to you. We're holding hands. You didn't have that before or maybe you did, I don't know. There are a million reasons why it could and should and would work between us. I'm sure there are a few reasons it wouldn't, couldn't and shouldn't. I'd rather look at the glass half full than half empty, and I'd rather try than wonder."

Okay, she'd give him that. She admired that about him too. He could look at the bright, possible side of things, and there were times where she could too when she was around him. "Well, and you did drive ten hours in the middle of the night and threaten to hogtie me if I didn't come along quietly. Coercion goes a long way, it seems."

"There is that. But for the record, baby, I didn't threaten to hogtie you. We can try that later though. I'm very good at ropin'."

"Two days isn't long enough to know, Justin." Her tone was once again serious.

"No, it's not. A year of talking, of learning to care, of weekends full of incredibly hot sex really makes me want to give it a shot, though."

"Why does it have to be at your place?"

"Because at your place you could retreat into your shell too easily. At my place, you'll be naked all day and night and unable to hide anywhere."

"I could be naked at my place too."

"Yeah, but it's not the same."

"How is it not the same?"

"You have neighbors and I don't have anyone for miles around. We can make all the noise we want. We can have sex outside in the yard. I can tie you to the old hitching post and spank you. I can let you be free to be the woman I've caught a glimpse of a few times. I can give you that at my place."

Ella had a feeling they were no longer talking about being naughty at his house. She had a feeling they were headed into the heart of things again. She didn't know if she could live up to what he thought of her, but she sure as hell needed to try. For both their sakes.

"I still can't believe you came for me."

"You didn't give me a choice."

And she hadn't. She knew it. "How much longer before we get there?"

"Oh just a couple of hours. Why? You need to stop? The next exit is pretty populated with stores and such. We can stretch our legs."

Was he always so kind, so giving, so accommodating? His care and concern amazed her. It wasn't something she was used to. She was the one who always made sure everyone else was taken care of and had everything they needed for their comfort. Justin, though, even with his overt maleness and his aggressive sexuality and his ruggedly handsome cowboy looks, he was the kindest, most caring man she could remember, save for her grandpa.

The thought of the only solid male figure in her life as she'd grown up made her smile. He'd have liked Justin a lot. He'd asked if she was sure as he walked with her down the aisle, and though she wasn't sure at all, she'd smiled at him and said yes so he wouldn't worry. He'd worried anyway until the day he died.

"Do you want me to stop here?"

"No, it's okay. I was just wondering if my bags were in a place I could reach them."

"Should be. I put them right behind the seat."

She tugged her hand from his hold and unbuckled her seatbelt. Pulling her knees under her, she knelt on the seat and leaned over the back of it. She had to move her laptop bag, but she got to the carry-on pretty easily. She unzipped the top and reached in for the item she needed.

She zipped the bag and started to turn around, but Justin's hand, cupping her ass over her skirt, stopped her. "What's wrong?"

"Nothing."

"Then why are you holding me in this position? I need to turn around and sit back down."

"I know. Just a second."

She looked over at him. "A second for what?"

"This." He flipped on the cabin light and flipped up the back of her skirt as they passed a couple of semis.

"Justin!" Embarrassment heated her skin, and she buried her face in her arms. The air horns from the trucks added further embarrassment to her predicament, and the smack that

Justin landed on her ass... "I can't believe you did that," she groaned.

"Sure you can. Wanna play some more? You could turn around and give them a real good show."

"No!"

Justin laughed and removed his hand, letting her skirt fall into place over her behind. She turned quickly and sat, crossing her arms tightly over her chest and tucking her chin. He reached over and ruffled her hair before grabbing a fistful and pulling lightly until she lifted her head. "Baby?"

"I just... I've never done anything like that before."

"You didn't do it. I did."

True, he had. "I know, but still."

"Upset?"

Was she? "Not really."

"Embarrassed?"

Very. "A little."

"Like it?"

She was afraid she did. "I think so."

"Good girl. I'll bring that vixen out in you."

And truth be told, she couldn't wait.

Chapter Four

"It's so dark out here."

"Yeah. I like it. Quiet too. I don't think I could live in the city for a long period of time."

They were on the small two-lane road headed toward his place. About ten miles back, Justin had pulled off the highway and begun the last leg of the road trip. He'd been driving something close to twenty hours, but given the woman at his side, it was worth every bit of tired eyes and aching ass from having been awake and sitting too damn long.

He could get home in the dark. He knew this road so well. Three more bumps in the pavement and he turned left onto the dirt lane leading up to the house. It was about a quarter-mile to his front door.

"How long have you lived out here?" Ella asked, staring out her window.

"All my life. I bought this part of the property and some cattle from my parents. It still runs as one big operation, but I keep whatever profit I make on this side. I usually just put it back into the upkeep."

The outline of the small clapboard house loomed ahead, and he parked the truck in front. There was no designated driveway or parking area and that was just fine with him. "Here we are. Home sweet home."

Ella leaned forward in her seat a little and squinted out the windshield. "Well from what I can see, it's a pretty little house."

"You'll see the outside tomorrow. Tonight though..." Justin turned off the ignition and climbed down out of the truck. He tried not to sound like a girl when he hit the ground and his legs wanted to give out as soon as he stood. He bent and flexed and reached as he stretched his body out. He loved his truck, but damn...

He walked around the front end to the passenger side and opened Ella's door. She turned to the side with her feet dangling over the edge of the seat. "Bunny slippers? Really?" Justin shook his head, but the smirk was firmly in place as he looked down at Ella's feet clad, not in the cute pink sandals she'd been wearing earlier, but in a pair of gray bunny slippers, complete with floppy bunny ears and what looked like a cotton tail at the back of the heel.

"Yes. Things were getting too serious in the truck there for a while."

"I know." And he did. He'd wanted, needed to lighten the mood for both of them. "That's why I flipped up your skirt for the truckers. But, bunny slippers?" Never in a million years would he have guessed her to be the bunny-slipper type. He thought those were reserved for giggly college girls at slumber parties.

"After I signed the divorce papers, a couple of friends came over and brought me wine, chocolate and these slippers. They told me that when things got too tense, too serious, too dramatic, or too emotional, put the slippers on to ease and lighten things up. That you couldn't be too much of any of those with bunny slippers."

Much as he hated to admit it... "I guess I can see that." She grinned, and he couldn't help but move in and kiss her pretty mouth.

"Thank you," she whispered when he pulled away a little.

"For what?" His hands gripped her hips, and he eased her to the ground.

"For not making fun of my slippers, for not...judging me."

His heart ached for the softness in her voice. "Baby, you know I don't judge you. Never have. Never will. Look—" he smoothed her hair back from her face, curving it over the shell of her ear, "—remember when I told you about Megan? The woman I lived with for a while?"

Confusion marred her brow for a moment but cleared soon enough. "Oh God, Justin. I'm so sorry. I'd forgotten all about her and... Oh damn, she left you for your friend."

"Yeah, she did. I asked her a few times why when I saw her after the fact, and she never gave me any solid answer. I only got some version of 'it just wasn't working out, Justin'. I would have done anything to change whatever she thought or felt was wrong, but she never gave me anything to go on. All I got was how sorry she was."

Ella nodded. "I remember now. I... Justin, how could you...?"

"Because you're not her, and I'm not him. If you hadn't left him when you did before we met, I don't know where we'd be or what would have happened, but I don't have to worry about that now because you and he are divorced and you're mine now."

"Yours?" She lifted a brow and another smile tugged at her lips.

"Yes. Mine. Until or if you ever give me a reason that you don't want to be. You'll be forced to give me a chance to change your mind, though."

Her eyes widened and the smile fully formed. "Forced? You mean with rope and spankings?"

"Maybe." Justin shrugged and started divesting her of the clothes she'd been wearing since he picked her up a little more than ten hours ago. "May include an anal hook, a saw horse, a ball gag." He slipped her shirt off her shoulders and bit back his own smile when she shook it all the way down her arms. He grabbed it before it hit the dirt and tossed it back into the cab of the truck.

"What if I'm extra determined not to be yours?" She steadied herself with her hands on his shoulders as he bent his knees and reached around behind her to unzip her skirt.

"Then I guess I'll have to employ a few other tactics." The skirt slipped down, and she stepped out of it for him. It joined her shirt inside the truck. He stood to his full height again and took her in...the lush curves of her hips and thighs, the roundedness of her breasts encased in pink lace, the dip of her waist. She was, in his opinion, fuckin' smokin' hot.

At his slow, up-and-down perusal, she let her hands drift over her body in an effort to cover her chest and her sex, but he snagged her wrists and shook his head. "Nope. No hiding yourself from me."

"I don't like being stared at like that."

"I don't know why the hell not, baby. You've never had a problem with me looking at you before. You didn't have a problem with the truckers getting an eyeful of your ass, either. I don't know what you think you're keepin' me from seein' but, no."

"Justin... " She turned her head to the side, breaking eye contact with him.

"No hiding your body from me."

"Or what?" she challenged. "You'll tie me up?"

"If that's what you want." He bent and softly nudged his shoulder into her soft belly, effectively lifting her over his shoulder.

"Justin! Put me down." She beat at his back with her fists and tried to find a way to push against his shoulders, but she couldn't.

Justin slowly backed away from the truck and kicked the door shut. "I will not. Now stop your fussin'."

"I'm too heavy for you to carry."

He took the steps up to the porch and fished the keys out of his front pocket. "Evidently not." And he took a nibble of the butt cheek closest to his face. She yelped and wiggled, so he did it again. "Hold still so I can unlock the door without dropping you."

She stilled immediately, and her chin rested against his back. "That definitely wouldn't set the right tone for the rest of the night."

A chuckle rumbled up from his chest. "It wouldn't. You're right about that."

He fumbled the key into the lock and got them into the house without dropping her. He kicked that door shut too and headed up the small staircase to the loft where he'd situated his bed. Not much else fit in the space itself, but a bathroom to the left was the size of a small bedroom and housed a closet for his clothing.

"What about my luggage and stuff?" she asked when he lowered her to the bed and followed her down.

He swallowed her sigh in a kiss as she sank into the very nice, very expensive mattress. His tongue tangled with hers, her legs tangled with his and she cradled him against her body much as she had back at the rest area.

He almost couldn't believe she was with him, beneath him in his bed. He'd never let on to her that he hadn't been sure she'd come along. Yet, she'd said yes.

It was wet and hot between her thighs, even through his jeans, and his cock was insistent that it be let out of his confinement and into the tightness he knew awaited him inside her. He tried to break the kiss so he could make his way down to her breasts, her belly, her pussy, but she wouldn't let him go, wriggling under him, as she tightened her hold and deepened her kiss.

Not that he really minded. He would happily stay right where he was for the next three days, but if he didn't at least let his dick out and start fucking her...

He worked his hands down under his body as best he could and lifted slightly, enough that he could work at his jeans. The backs of his fingers brushed against her heat and he let her know with a groan how much he liked it.

Pulling back to take a breath, he wondered if the look on his face matched the hunger on hers. It had to. His brain was going a mile a minute with only one thought—fuck her now. Fuck her now. Fuck. Her. Now. It wasn't romantic. It wasn't sexy by romance standards. It wasn't even erotic. No, it was pure animal need thrumming through his blood. He didn't need slow, and judging by the insistent humping she was doing, she wasn't looking for slow either.

Her next words confirmed it.

"Hurry, Justin."

"Hurryin', minx." And his fingers fumbled with the button fly of the fresh jeans he'd put on before they left the rest stop. It was his usual choice, but damn if he wasn't considering all zippers from now on.

"I'm too old to be any kind of minx," she grumped, arching her back and pushing her chest into his.

He sat back on his knees, his fingers protesting the loss of her heat, but they were able to pop the buttons on his jeans much faster. His cock popped out through the opening at the same time she was able to get her bra off. Naked. The woman was naked, and though he'd seen her partially naked at her apartment and in the bed of the truck, it wasn't the same.

He reached over and switched on the lamp, bathing the loft in a soft glow. She blinked rapidly at him until her eyes adjusted to the small change in light. Her color heightened.

"Hi," she said quietly.

"Hi, baby." He leaned down and kissed the tip of her nose. "You're not too old to be anything," he whispered before leaning over again and opening the drawer in the nightstand. The two boxes of condoms he'd purchased before heading to Alabama were opened and ready for use, and he pulled a strip out. "Least of all my minx."

She took it from him and tore one foil packet away from the rest. "Here, let me." She ripped it open, took the condom out, and before he could settle against her thighs again, she had the rubber rolled over his cock and was stroking him in long, slow motions, squeezing tightly as she got to the base and closing the ring of her thumb and forefinger as she got to the extra-sensitive tip.

Justin tried not to thrust his hips, tried not to hurry the pleasure her hand was bringing him, but soon he wasn't going to be able to hold back. She altered the pressure of her hand, loosening her hold on him to a near feather-light touch. It wasn't enough. She was teasing him, and when he thought to warn her about it, she gripped the shaft in her fist again. Sweat broke out on his brow and his breathing picked up. He curled his fingers into his palms against his thighs to keep from brushing hers away and angled down so he could plunge deep inside her.

It was when she brought her other hand up between his legs and cupped his balls in her palm that he did lose his tenuous hold on control. "Ella... " Her name was barely out of his mouth before his hands wrapped around her wrists and pinned them to the bed. He lowered himself to her opening and pushed inside. "Ella," he said again, this time as a whispered, thankful prayer that she was there with him.

Then he fucked her.

It lacked grace and elegance. It lacked romance and tenderness. It lacked everything a gentleman should do for the woman of his dreams once he had her in bed... Well, most everything. It didn't lack passion or heat or lust or need. No, this fucking had all that in abundance.

His hips pressed forward and back in a piston motion. His eyes stared into hers. His palms were clasping her wrists so tight he could feel her pulse beating through her skin into him. And his cock...his cock was in heaven, surrounded by throbbing, pulsating heat.

"Kiss me," she pleaded.

He did, lowering his head, his tongue touching her lips just as she began to open them. Her gaze locked with his and it was the most intense, intimate kiss he'd ever shared with a woman. They never shut their eyes, never broke the contact, even when she wrapped her legs around his hips and slid them to the middle of his back, lifting her ass just slightly off the bed.

The kiss was unhurried, but full of every ounce of his desire for her. Her thoughts, her needs...all were visible in her eyes. He twined his tongue around hers, pulling it deeper, harder, and the green of her gaze darkened. He read the urgency, felt the tensing of her body and for a moment, he thought she would close her eyes, unable to hold onto the intensity...

He shifted, bringing one hand up to close around her throat. Not tight, but just enough pressure, and he saw the heat spike in her eyes. He'd done this to her once before, this mimic of a collar around her throat, this mimic of ownership and her arousal had kicked up just as it did now. Her freed hand came up to wrap around his wrist, her hold just as tight if not tighter on him than his on her.

His lips hovered over hers, breath mingled, gazes still locked. Her pulse thrummed beneath his thumb and his body pumped between her thighs.

Her legs gripped his sides and she pulled herself up, fucking him. She liked this power, this freedom to let go and give as good as she got. He understood that rawness, that delight, that holding of everything vital in the palm of your hand.

"Take it, baby. Take me," he growled against her parted lips.

She licked his mouth and bounced on the bed, screwing his cock. Her nipples scraped his chest and he dipped his head, sinking his teeth into her chin, drawing an animalistic moan from her. This was why he had wanted to wait until he got her back to his place before he had sex with her. He wanted her to let go in his bed. He wanted this image of her open and giving and taking and sharing, imprinted on his brain.

She was allowed to be uninhibited here with him, and he knew she'd feel it and hoped she'd embrace it. In that moment, she had and she was, and he was happy to be the vessel she rode to the end.

"More, Ella. Give me more," he whispered against the cleft in her chin before licking up from it to the beads of perspiration on her upper lip.

"I..." She gulped for air.

"I know. You're so good, baby. You're so, so good."

Her smile was beautiful and bashful and sexy as hell. He pressed her harder into the bed with his hands on her wrist and throat, and his hips started to meet her upward thrusts with his own downward strokes. He needed to come.

And he needed to come now. He needed to relieve the pressure in his balls, the tension in his gut and come so hard that he would be the one bouncing on the bed.

Then her smile turned wicked. Dark. Her eyes shifted and changed, the color nearly swallowed by the black of her pupils. His aggression turned her on, always had, he knew, but to see it again, to see how it transformed her, the rough fuck, the hard shoves opening her, widening her, preparing her. He lusted for that look, that fire.

"C'mon, Justin, fuck me."

Her voice dropped in sex, becoming throaty, raspy, and it skittered across his nerves. If there was a woman whose sex he was meant for, it was hers. Every hot, sinfully blessed inch of it.

"More, please. Give me more."

The plea was in her eyes as well as on her lips. Her cunt dripped on his cock and soaked down to his balls. He was a goner. Completely.

A shout rumbled up from his chest and echoed around the room as he came. He felt his fingers tighten around her throat, felt her nails dig into his wrist as his semen filled the rubber. God, he wanted to come inside her...

"Yes," she sighed.

His vision refocused on her face and he saw that beautiful smile, that well-used look suffuse her eyes. He let go of her throat and her wrist where he held her and slid down her body, his dick sliding out, semi-hard, and his lips latched onto her clit, sucking it for all he was worth.

She gripped his hair and pushed his face against her pussy. Nowhere else in the world he'd rather be as his teeth nibbled on her, working her over, begging her without words to cream for him.

"Justin," she breathed.

He nodded, and his chin brushed against her wetness.

"Jus...tin..." she panted and tightened her hold on his hair.

He slid his arms under her knees and pulled her legs over his shoulders, buried his face in her and feasted. He didn't do this with finesse or gentleness either. He didn't do it with teasing or light little licks meant to drive her higher.

No, he devoured her, ate at her as a starving man, feasted and savored. She was sensitive and tender, alight with an arousal he'd not felt from a woman in years. He did this to her, drove her to reach for those peaks of pleasure.

She quivered around his tongue as he licked through her folds, as he licked at the wetness, as he tasted every inch of her slit splayed before him. The muscles in her thighs and the muscles in her lower belly clenched as she strained around him, grasping for the orgasm.

She curved inward, lifting her shoulders and head off the bed and cried out, humping the hell out of his face as she rode out the orgasm flowing through her. He didn't stop eating at her and she didn't stop fucking him.

"More. Jus, pl-please."

He shifted his head and pushed his chin against her clit and rubbed hard, making her shake anew as she continued to come, as she gushed against his new sheets.

She fell back onto the mattress almost immediately and he dipped his face, savoring the juices she'd given him then slid up and kissed her, sharing it with her. This intimacy, this sharing of her cream was something he longed to do with his own too. He wanted to share the taste with her, especially the taste of them together.

"Do you know what I just realized," he whispered into her ear. She only shook her head as a response. "I just realized that this entire time through the kissing and fucking and making you squirt in my bed, you've been wearing those damn bunny slippers."

Justin slid back onto the bed and pulled Ella close after getting up to dispose of the condom and cleaning himself up and then her. He'd laid a towel over the wet spot after she declared she wouldn't be sleeping on it. He'd laughed but agreed that neither would he. The towel covering it was the compromise. "I suppose we could get up and I could show you around the house," he said as he settled in. Of course, if she said yes, he'd get up again without a word of complaint.

"It can wait until morning." She yawned and stretched, pressing her toes against his legs.

"You sure?"

She snuggled deeper into his side. "Yeah, I'm sure."

"Hungry at all? You said the last time you ate was just before I got there. That was a long time ago."

This time she stifled a yawn against his chest. "I'll be good until I wake up. Of course, if you don't have coffee, we're going to have issues."

He remembered her addiction to coffee. Coffee whore, she'd once coined herself. He rather liked both parts of that. "I've got plenty. I stocked up before I left to come get you."

"Why? I'm sure you have a store or a coffee shop we could have run to."

"I was prepared to tie you to the bed for a few days if you proved to be difficult and I knew without the lure of coffee, I'd have a very hard time convincing you of anything."

"Justin, really. When have you ever known me to be anything but docile and compliant?"

He pulled away slightly and looked down at her at the same moment she looked up at him. "Seriously?" The look she gave him was a very horrible interpretation of docile and compliant. She was more mischievous and full-of-imp inspiration and she wasn't fooling him for a second.

"I'm very accommodating. I came here of my own free will, didn't I?"

Really? She was going to bat her eyelashes at him? "Only after I showed you the rope and told you I'd tie you up until you said yes."

"And yet you still tied me up in the back of the truck."

Yes, he had. He couldn't wait to tie her up again. The bright green rope against her pale skin and nearly same color as the lace of her bra... He couldn't have planned that better if he'd known what she was going to be wearing. The way she moved within her bonds, the way the rope stretched and her muscles strained... She was the hottest woman and most of the time she didn't even see it. "Don't act as if you didn't like it."

She smiled and laid her head back to his chest. "Thank you for coming to get me, Justin."

"Like I said before, you didn't give me much choice." Justin tightened his arms around her and nuzzled his face into her hair.

Going and getting her, making her understand that she was wanted and desired, that he needed her in his life was just the tip of the iceberg of what he needed to do to show her that she could lean on him, trust him to meet her halfway in life and not shut her out.

His Ella needed affection, needed romance, needed to be manhandled more than once in a while. She needed to be treated like a woman, strong and independent. She needed to be treated as a sexual fantasy come to life, a precious slut, a desired submissive. He could give her those things if she'd trust him enough to let him into more than just her body.

He felt her go limp against him, felt her soft breath even out against his skin and her hand relax against his stomach. She was sleeping. He'd waited months for this, for this moment when he could hold her in his arms again as she slept. Of course, he still had to go back outside and bring in her luggage and laptop bag, but overall, it was what he'd waited months for.

Sex with her for certain, time with her, talking with her, all of it, but holding her while she slept, holding her when she was the most defenseless and vulnerable, that's what he'd wanted, what he felt she deserved.

He slowly slid his arm from under her neck and eased his body away from hers. A small whimper escaped her lips and a slight frown marred her brow, but she didn't wake. For a split second he started to pick up his jeans, but why? He lived in the middle of nowhere. No one would see him unless they were trespassing on his property, and well, that'd be their own damn fault if they caught him in all his glory.

He took the stairs quietly and slipped on a pair of flip-flops before letting himself out the front door. The moon lit the yard and stable nearly as bright as day, and the stars winked in the night sky. He wondered if Ella had ever seen a sky as clear and dark as the Texas sky was right then? He'd take her out back tomorrow night and sit on the swing with her, hold her hand and just be there with her as she gazed up. She would love it. He had no doubt about that.

He opened the passenger door to the truck and grabbed her bags, careful not to bang either one against the front of his thighs, then set one down so he could shut the truck door with as minimal noise as possible. From the front seat, he got her purse and discarded clothes before gathering everything up again and heading to the house.

He left the laptop bag on the couch in the living room along with her purse. He took her other bags up the stairs and set them both against the wall near the side of the bed she slept on. After a trip into the bathroom to pee and brush his teeth, he crawled into the bed and gathered her in his arms again.

His eyes were already closing when she sighed and nuzzled her face against his chest before rolling over to face away from him. He smiled and eased himself close until he was spooned against her, an exhausted and sated sleep soon taking him.

Chapter Five

Ella rolled over and spied the rather large cup of coffee. As she looked at it from her position on the bed and then inched up closer on her belly, she realized it wasn't a cup at all, but a soup bowl with a handle. She wondered for a moment if it would be considered Texas size?

"What a sweet, wonderful man," she intoned aloud to the empty room.

Sitting up, she propped a pillow against the solid wood headboard and reached for the coffee. From her current angle, the bowl wasn't much smaller than the tray it sat on. There were two shot glasses of creamer and a spoon as well. She couldn't have been more touched, and sudden emotion clogged her throat and made her chest ache.

She blinked her eyes rapidly, swearing she had something in them before actually picking up the cup and one of the shot glasses. Emptying one, she swirled the cream through the coffee and tasted, screwing up her face at the still too-strong flavor and emptied the second shot glass of cream.

Yes, a giant cup required four full ounces of cream instead of just two. She took a sip and let the caffeine do its magic on her tired and not-quite-awake system. She became more aware of things quickly though, the silence in the house being the biggest thing. Where was he?

There was no sound coming from downstairs. It didn't surprise her that nothing had awoken her, being as tired and worn out as she was from the trip, the sex and the orgasms.

However, the silence was beginning to make her nervous. She didn't know why exactly. She was used to being alone and it had never bothered her before, but for some reason, maybe because she was in a house that wasn't her own, she didn't have that same peace that solitude usually brought in its wake.

She slid her leg over to the side of the bed he'd slept on and it was cold as ice. He must have been up for a few hours and, looking around, she didn't see a clock anywhere, but she did see her purse sitting in a ladder-back chair in the corner. Her suitcase sat against the loft railing. She'd bet her laptop bag was somewhere around too, and if she looked on the floor beside the bed... Yep, her bunny slippers sat there, waiting for her feet to slide right on in.

That *thing* was back in her eyes again, making her blink rapidly to get it out.

She lay in his bed, drinking the coffee he'd made for her, feeling the aches in her body and the light ache in her neck where he'd held her down. It felt like a bruise and she'd be curious to see if there was one, but she doubted it. He didn't squeeze hard enough, but the slight tenderness when she touched where his thumb had been... She smiled.

God, she loved the way he pinned her down, held her. It was a possession of her.

They'd toyed with some light control play over the months. He'd tied her up, but so loosely she could get out with little more than a twist of her wrist. He'd spanked her a bit, enough for it to sting, not enough for it to mark. But the kiss before she'd left the room the last time to head home had been tender and rough by turns, possessive and freeing too. He'd pushed

73

her up against the hotel room door and gripped her throat in his hand, pressing his body so hard into her that it had lifted her up on her toes.

She'd felt his hold on her all the way home that day and every day since. She had no idea what she was doing here with him now, what pipedream she might be living or buying into. Sure, they'd gotten along well and they had a sexual chemistry that defied anything in her previous experience, before and including her ex.

Those feelings, those desires, those pleasures were things her life had been missing since the day she'd gotten married and she hadn't realized it. She hadn't realized exactly what she was missing, what her mind and her gut had been trying to tell her before she walked down the aisle…

Justin had shown her, had opened her eyes. First through words and then through actions. She hadn't ever imagined she could have a life with him, and she still didn't know if it was possible. There were questions and obstacles and their ages and…. How much did all that baggage matter, she wondered as she caressed the pillow where he'd slept? He knew her shit, all of it. She knew his too, or at least most of it. And she knew if she brought up the age difference to him, he'd tan her hide until she couldn't sit.

They'd never discussed the—she had to count it out on her fingers, the ones not holding the coffee—ten or eleven year gap between their birthdays. It hadn't bothered her before and she couldn't think of a reason for it to bother her now. Maybe she was just looking for more excuses for it not to work because that was easier than taking a chance on all the reasons it could work.

Besides, she smiled, she was in his bed, all the way in Dallas because he'd had enough of being without her.

And that he'd gone to Birmingham for her.... He'd been right though. She wouldn't answer him with more than general statements. She wouldn't talk to him about personal stuff anymore. She kept putting him off about how she was really feeling, what she was really thinking, and their friendship, their relationship was worth more than that. He'd always allowed her and encouraged her to talk about anything and she'd shut him out. The only choices he'd had were to either let her be or show up on her doorstep.

But she'd never thought he'd actually take the latter option. It wasn't as if she'd said put up or shut up. No, she hadn't said anything at all and in his mind, she was worth trying to salvage something.

No guy had ever come after her, ever chased her, ever thrown her over his shoulder like a caveman. No guy had ever brought her coffee in bed.

"Damn," she whispered.

She flipped back the sheet and slid her feet into her slippers before setting the coffee down on the tray. She felt a little nervous walking across the loft naked, but that was the only way to get to the bathroom and then her suitcase.

Once some necessities were taken care of, she would get dressed. She hadn't packed clothes for roaming around a ranch. If she'd thought about it at the time, she'd have thrown a pair of jeans and a T-shirt into her suitcase before leaving the apartment. As it was, she had a pair of brown slacks to go with a cream camisole and matching short-sleeve, light-weight sweater and a pair of black slacks and a pink, black and white striped button-down-the-front blouse. She had work clothes and yoga clothes as well, but nothing meant for wandering around a Texas ranch. Not to mention, she'd only brought sandals and heels.

She had no idea what to do, what to put on to go look for him, but standing there naked looking through her suitcase wasn't helping. Making up her mind to don the brown pants and white sweater outfit, she quickly went back to the bathroom for a shower before getting dressed. She hadn't brought shampoo or body wash because she used what was in the hotels and was lucky Justin had regular all-purpose shampoo and everyday soap so she wouldn't go around smelling like a man. She wrapped her towel-dried hair up in a ponytail and brushed her teeth, debating on whether a little makeup was called for or not.

"Gonna have to get you some boots to wear around here. Can't have you walking in those cutesy shoes and fuck-me-heels all the time."

She yelped, and her hand flew to the flesh over her heart as she looked over at him. She hadn't heard him coming, hadn't heard... Her gaze immediately began to drink him in. Damn, he looked good all dirty and sweaty in faded jeans that looked about worn through in all the right places and a dark blue T-shirt with faded writing on the front. A tan cowboy hat was plastered to his head and his brown boots were scuffed with dirt and scrapes and well worn. He was every inch a cowboy. He was every inch her cowboy. The reality of that hit her square in the stomach. "What about bunny slippers?"

"Nah, we'll save those. You like to wear those when we fuck."

His outright crudeness should have probably shocked her, but it didn't. "Yeah, okay. Plus, I don't want to get them dirty."

"No more than they already are after last night. Probably made the poor bunnies blush."

"Eh." She shrugged. "They're bunnies. They're used to such things."

He grabbed her by the waist and hauled her against him.. "They better not have seen any action before us last night."

The look in his eyes wasn't a happy, teasing look. Jealousy? It never occurred to her that Justin would ever be jealous of her or that he would think she would have been with someone else all these months. She'd been asked out, but she'd always said no. Should she date others? Should she play the field a bit? Maybe it wasn't just Justin who could make her feel the things he did.

As she stood against him, with his arms holding her tight and imprisoned against his body... No, no one else would be able to do for her what he did, and she didn't want to date a bunch of guys in search of something she already had.

"No. No one else has seen me naked with bunny slippers. No one else has had sex with me while I wore my bunny slippers. Only you."

"Good. I might not be too sure about the kinkiness of bunny slippers and sex, but I sure don't want anyone else seeing how sexy and cute you are wearing them when you're naked and wet and have your legs spread wide."

He bent his head and nuzzled her neck, tipping the hat off his head in the process. She caught it before it dropped farther down and placed it on her own head. He smelled like the outdoors—grass, dirt, horses. The ends of his hair dripped sweat and his neck was streaked with dirt, but she didn't care. She slid her hands under his T-shirt, flicked his nipples with her fingers and was rewarded with a bite to her earlobe before sliding her hands around to his back and down to the waistband of his jeans.

He was lean, his body honed from hard work and manual labor, not built in a gym. She'd always liked that about him— that he didn't work behind a desk. It wasn't that she had anything against men in offices; she just liked the blue-collar men, the ones who had physical jobs best. She felt safe with men like that. She felt they could take care of her physically, take care of her if something went wrong and she was in need.

She also realized that that probably sounded silly, but men like Justin with jobs and hobbies such as he had turned her on.

"What're you thinkin'?"

"Huh?" she uttered against his throat.

"Your breathing has gotten all hot and heavy."

"Uh-huh." She nodded and licked a trail up from his Adam's apple to his chin.

"You're playin' with fire, baby." But he slid his hand up into her ponytail just the same.

"You started it." Ella stood on tiptoes and continued licking her way up his chin until she could reach his mouth. He met her in a swirl of tongues. His jeans were loose enough she could slide her hands down inside the back of them to grab and squeeze his ass. His—"You're not wearing any underwear," she whispered against his mouth, continuing to kiss and nibble on his lips.

"Nope," he whispered back, allowing her all the freedom she wanted to explore him.

"Naughty boy."

"You should know."

"Well," she said as she slid her hands around to the front of his jeans, smiling when he sucked in his already flat stomach. She felt the fluttering of his muscles against her fingers and gave a soft purr of delight. She loved the effect she had on him because it mirrored the effect he had on her, "since you're *sans* underwear, you should be *sans* jeans too."

Buttons were popped open and denim was urged down his hips just enough for his cock to spring out, the head peeking from the surrounding skin. She wanted to lean over and slide her tongue over the tip, wrap her hand around the shaft and slide the foreskin farther down so she could suck him but good.

"I was right, huh?"

She didn't need to be reminded what he was talking about. "Yeah, you were right." One time early on, he'd told her that once she got a taste and feel for an uncircumcised penis, she'd never want to go back to one that was circumcised. He hadn't been kidding in his boasting and cockiness. She hadn't known what the difference was and because they'd always used condoms during sex, he said she hadn't gotten the full benefit yet of him being uncut.

She hoped one day to find out every inch of the full benefit.

As it was, she didn't think she'd ever get enough of looking at the uncut perfection. His was the first and only uncut penis she'd ever played with or had the pleasure of and she loved it. He seemed to take great pride in the fact he wasn't circumcised. The extra-sensitive head when she touched him, the way the foreskin slid back and forth when he thrust in her hand was an added sexiness she hadn't expected, like an erotic game of peek-a-boo.

She started to kneel. She wanted a taste of him, but he held her up and shook his head. "No time for that, baby. I need to bend you over the railing there and fuck you silly."

Ella pouted but wasn't a bit disappointed. Him fucking her was turning out to be a necessity. Once a day might be enough for right now, but if she spent much more time with him, it wasn't going to be.

He let her go, and she walked over to the log railing of the loft and looked over the edge. Directly below her was a brown couch with tapestry-covered pillows. She couldn't make out the designs but thought they were horse scenes. In the corner of the couch was her laptop bag.

Justin's hand on her hip brought her immediately back to him and what he wanted, what she wanted. She started to take her sweater off, but he stayed her hand there too. "Nope. Just push the pants down enough that I can get to you, and you need to hurry."

She looked over her shoulder to find him slowly stroking the cock she wanted to be on her knees sucking, and for a minute, she thought to do just that no matter what he said, but the look in his eyes kept her on her feet, freeing the snap and lowering the zipper of her brown slacks.

He had them down to her knees and her bent forward before she could take another breath. She heard the foil of a condom rip, heard him mutter how he hated using the damn things, heard his sigh and hiss of pleasure when he reached between her legs and found her, "Wet. Damn, you're so fucking wet, baby. Spread as wide as you can for me."

She did, as wide as her pants around her knees would allow. He splayed her pussy open with his fingers and pushed inside her hard, quick, and she had to grab onto the railing to steady herself.

"That's my girl." He tugged on her ponytail and gripped her hip and fucked her.

His hat was still on her head and his boots scuffed on the floor as he rode her into the wood that kept her from tumbling down.

He filled her completely, and the animalistic grunts and groans that escaped her left a lot to be desired of a lady. The way he held her, pummeled into her, kept her from being able to do much more than take what he was giving, submit to what he was doing.

She couldn't have been happier.

But she could surprise him by shifting back up on her tiptoes and leaning forward slightly. Her ass pushed against his groin, and he slammed into her harder. "Oh yeah, baby, God, that feels good."

Head pulled back by her hair, he stepped closer into her space, thrust short and shallow and let go of her hip to slide his hand up the front of her body, squeeze her tit through her now mangled and dirt-stained sweater, and up higher until his fingers could slide between her lips and into her mouth.

"Suck," he ground out.

And so she sucked. Three fingers invaded her mouth, pressed on her tongue. His lips skated down the side of her face and still he fucked her, the front of his thighs rubbing up against the back of hers.

"Yeah, you like it, don't you?"

She did. The harder and rougher he treated her in sex, the kinky paths he led her down to explore, the more special the tender, loving moments became and she wanted it all, from one extreme to the other. He knew what he was doing when he came for her. He knew he could give her everything she needed and wanted. He knew how to use her body to his advantage. He knew her better than she knew herself at times, especially in this area of sex and possession. He trusted her more than she trusted herself too.

He pulled his fingers from her mouth and wedged them down between her body and the railing. They slid against her clit with ease and as Justin stepped back again, started thrusting hard and sure again, he rubbed and manipulated the little nerve bundle on the outside and rubbed against and manipulated the corresponding spot inside her with the length of his cock.

"You look good in my hat, baby. You're gonna look good coming while wearing it too, huh?"

"Yeah," she breathed, her mouth suddenly parched, her lips dry.

"Then let me have it. Let me see you come wearing my cowboy hat."

He pressed and he pulled. He stroked and he rubbed, coaxing her to start reaching for it. She held onto the wooden railing, picked a spot to focus on below, and lost herself in the feel of cock inside her, fingers fondling her.

"That's it. Yeah, baby, give it to me."

His voice was distant, but his breath was hot on her neck, and she shivered from the moist heat.

Heat. It filled her up from the inside out until she was perspiring from the top of her head to the soles of her feet in her little sandals. He slid easily in and out of her pussy, spreading her wetness, and then she was gone, flying over the edge, coming on his fingers, his cock, and he was pushing her for more, urging her to keep going, to keep squeezing him.

He croaked out her name, grunted and stilled, all but the jerk of his hips as his balls emptied inside the condom. She pulsed around him and he twitched against her walls. He let go of her hair, kissed the sensitive spot between shoulder and neck, then removed his hand from between her legs and hugged his body to hers.

Ella lowered her heels to the floor, and he leaned her forward until she was resting against the rail.

"Damn, I think you're trying to kill me," he uttered into her hair.

"I don't think that's true at all. I think it's you trying to kill me." She took deep breaths, one right after the other, trying to calm her heartbeat.

"I need you, Ella."

She stopped breathing at those four words, muttered so softly she barely heard them over the thundering cadence of her heart. "Jus—"

"No. Don't fight this. Just let me need you. Has anyone ever? Has anyone ever needed you like this? Just please let me."

How could she say no to that? "Okay."

The late afternoon sun beat on his shoulders. The one fence post had been repaired, the horses brushed, the few cows that had wandered over to his side of the land herded back to his parents' side and the stable door fixed. He was worn out, but damn, at the same time, he'd never felt more alive and full of energy. He'd done more today than he'd intended to do, including changing out the spark plugs and oil filter on the old Ford pickup they used specifically for ranch work. His brother was finishing up college at Tech but was around as much as he could to help.

Justin was grateful for it too. His brother helping out allowed Justin the chance to take off and kidnap Ella. He laughed. Kidnap. He didn't exactly take her against her will. He'd just made it impossible for her to refuse. He simply put something she wanted in front of her and in a roundabout way, dared her to say no.

His brother had come for a long weekend and watched over Justin's horses and worked around the place a little while Justin went to Alabama. He couldn't begin to describe the feeling he'd had when he woke up at the ass crack of dawn and she was there, in his bed, snoring soundly. He loved her and he wanted her with him, in bed and out. He just had to get inside her walls and figure out what she was running from or trying to protect herself against.

Slipping his hat off his head, he wiped at the sweat on his brow with the back of his arm. Summer was coming hard and fast, and the heat felt as if it were going to be worse than last year. Though it seemed every summer got hotter and hotter and every winter colder and colder.

The back door to the house slammed shut, and he turned his head. Ella. Justin grinned and stared. She set a picnic basket down at the edge of the steps and then made her way toward him, carrying a large, handled thermos. He'd loaned her a T-shirt that stretched tight across her breasts and hips. She still wore the same brown pants she'd had on earlier that morning when he'd been unable to keep himself from bending her over.

"We definitely need to get you some boots," he said for the second time that day. She stepped up to him and handed him the red drink cooler. He flipped the pour-spout lid and tilted his head back, only to lower it again. "This water?"

"Yes."

"Good." He tilted his head back again and lifted the water jug up and poured. The icey liquid slid over his face and down his neck, his shoulders, his back and his chest. He stood there for a few seconds, reveling in the coolness under the sun. He slowly lowered the thermos back to his side. "Move away."

He waited and hoped she'd done as he said before he lowered his head and shook it, slinging water in every direction. Running his hands through his hair, slicking it back off his forehead, he opened his eyes to see her staring at him as if he were going to be her next meal. She licked her lips, and he wasn't even sure she realized she'd done it as she then lifted her thumb to her mouth and slid the tip between her teeth.

"Stop looking at me like that."

"Can't," she mumbled around the digit she was nibbling on.

"Why?" He didn't mind. He liked that she found him sexy, that she liked looking at him because he damn sure liked looking at her. Curves and valleys and strength and those green eyes that had haunted his dreams for months and that often had him waking up with his dick in his hand, stroking come up through the shaft.

"Don't know really. You're just... I can't stop."

"Well, try." Sternness with her was always going to be a problem. He might like to think he could be stern and firm with her, but he knew he wasn't fooling anyone, especially himself. She had him and his cock wrapped around her pretty little fingers. He could give it the old college try though. "Dirty as I am, I'm not aimin' to roll around in the mud with you. So, wipe that look off your face."

She raked him one more time with her gaze, starting at his feet and slowly moving up his legs, stopping at the juncture of his thighs. The longer she stared, the harder he got. He was going to find himself rolling around in the mud with her if she didn't knock off that lusting perusal.

"Ella, I said cut it out. I ain't a piece of meat." He tried for affronted, offended, something to get her to look up in his face instead of at the tented denim. He didn't pull it off.

She smiled slow and sure. "Yeah, you are."

Justin laughed. Okay, he was. And he'd gladly be her hunk of Grade A Prime any day because he loved that she was feeling good and open enough, safe enough to ogle him. He'd always thought if he could just get her alone for a while, just get her out of her element, she would blossom. He'd also thought if he got her alone, she'd wear his ass out with sex long before she was ready to stop.

He was good with that. But right now, he was hungry and tired of being in the sun. He wanted a shower, clean clothes, food...then Ella on her knees. Or maybe he wanted a shower, Ella on her knees, clean clothes and food. Then again, he could just want Ella on her knees, followed by both of them in the shower, both of them naked after, sharing that picnic she'd brought outside.

Swirling the rest of the water in the thermos, he grit his teeth against what he was about to do. She wasn't paying attention. Her stare kept traveling between his abs and his cock. She never saw him unscrew the top and drop it on the ground. She never saw him lift the jug and hold the bottom in his palm. She never saw it coming at all until the water hit her, soaking her face, her hair and the T-shirt she wore.

She sputtered, and he laughed.

"Wha—Justin..."

"I told you to stop that."

She wiped water from her face and he helped by slicking her hair back, just as he had his own. "I can't help it if you're so good looking. Go get ugly or something and I won't gawk."

He pressed a kiss to her soaking wet head and turned her so they could walk back to the house with his arm around her. He even tried to keep from looking down at her nipples, which were trying to poke holes in the shirt she wore. Obviously, he wasn't successful. "I don't want to get ugly. I like you gawking at me, but I have other plans for us for today that don't include a mud bath."

"What other plans?"

"Well, a shower, food...and...other things you'll just have to wait and find out about."

"But I don't want to wait."

Her pout was beautiful. "Tough, baby. You made me wait for months. You can wait a couple of hours."

"Mean, cowboy. You're just plain mean."

"I'm anything but mean. I'm cruel. I'm teasing. I'm dirty and I'm kinky. I'm even playful, loving. I can definitely be a hard ass, but I am never mean." Each word had been punctuated with him backing her up step by step until she was pressed against the kitchen door.

Her eyes grew wide, and she licked her full, pretty lips. Justin lowered his head, thought to kiss her, breathe her in. He watched as the pulse in her neck kicked up speed. Her eyes started to get heavy with arousal, dilated as he kept her hanging as to what his intentions were. Up until that moment, he hadn't known, but now with her desire for his kiss increasing, he knew exactly what he was going to do.

He leaned in a little closer, his lips right there, just about to touch hers and she reached for it, tilted her head up a scant inch for it...

Justin lifted his head and took a measured half step back. "I have plans for you, baby, but first I have plans to take a shower and get this grime off my body."

Ella just stared up at him, disbelief written all over her face. It took her a couple of minutes, maybe less to compose herself, but then she drew herself up and away from the door, stepped toward him and poked him in the chest. "Mean."

She stomped around him and down into the dusty yard, and then proceeded to stomp her way, as best she could in her little sandals, to where he'd dropped the thermos and lid. She bent, snatched them up, and all the while, muttered to herself. He couldn't hear it, didn't want to, but she was the most adorable woman when she was riled up. He liked her. Damn, he liked her so much it hurt his gut sometimes.

"You should think about getting out of that wet shirt. Don't want you to catch cold," he offered when she stomped back up on to the porch.

"I don't have another shirt. I wasn't packed for this kind of thing. I wasn't packed to spend a few days on a ranch. I was packed to spend a few days in New Orleans before the beginning of my training class."

"I could loan you another shirt or...."

She walked into his house just like she owned it. God, he loved that. He wanted to share it with her, share ownership with her. Hell, he just wanted to fucking own her. Every smile, every tear, every laugh, every pain, every orgasm. Everything about her he wanted to own and possess and devour. He'd never considered himself of caveman quality, of woman-mine mentality, but she brought out that side of him and he was hard pressed to argue against it.

Oh he was a kinky cuss and would share her in sex play if they both wanted it, but there'd be no one spending the night and Ella would always come home with him to sleep in their bed. With him.

"Or?"

He followed her inside but didn't bother to close the door behind him. Despite the heat outside, it was a gorgeous day and there was a light breeze. He stopped in his tracks and looked down at the dirt he'd brought in. Damn. The woman would make him forget his own name if he wasn't careful.

He backtracked and shucked his boots outside on the porch by the door and walked back in. She was standing by the sink with her arms crossed over her wet chest. Those nipples were still poking at the front of his shirt. His mouth watered to take one in his mouth and suckle until she was writhing enough that he could put her up on the coun—

"Stop that."

He looked up to find her wagging a finger at him. He bit back a smile and nodded. "Right. I'm going for a shower and you...yeah, you're coming with me."

He snagged her hand and pulled her along behind. "You never answered the or, Justin."

Or? Or, or, or? Oh. "Well, I believe getting you in the shower with me is answering it."

She stopped walking, forcing him to stop to. Her lips were pursed, her eyes narrowed. "Maybe I don't want to get into the shower with you."

"Liar."

She flushed after a second or two. "Ass."

He grinned. "Yep."

He tugged lightly and she pouted but followed. Yeah, life with her would be a treat. Now all he had to do was convince her to give it a try with him, but first, he needed to get her all hot and bothered and slippery wet between her thighs, that's when all her defenses were down, when she was open and giving. He wanted her on the edge, on that precipice where anything was possible, where she'd agree to anything if he'd just hold her right there, if he'd just keep her right there where her body quivered and all she could see and feel was pleasure.

He wasn't above manipulation to get her to see him, to need him. But he'd never trick her. It was all her choice, all her decision. He just wanted a fair shake, a fair try.

"Justin?"

He stopped halfway up the steps and turned around. She had that dreamy, lusty look in her eyes again. She'd been staring at his ass. "Naughty girl."

She nodded. "Can you take your jeans off?"

"What? Here?" He tried for affronted, again, but knew he failed.

She nodded again. "Uh-huh."

He let go a pretty good but fake annoyed sigh, which didn't faze her a bit, and made a big show of snapping buttons from their holes along his fly. Her green eyes darkened, and she licked her full bottom lip with the tip of her tongue.

Justin was at a bit of a loss as to what had gotten into her. She'd never looked at him like a piece of meat before today, at least not to the extent she was now or back out in the yard. "Ella."

Her head snapped up. "What?"

He laughed and pushed his jeans down his legs to his ankles, stood tall and held his arms out to his sides. His cock was harder than a hammer, and the tip peeked out from the foreskin. The air that blew across it from the room made him tingle, but the way she looked at him, as though he were her last meal, made the tingle go away.

She took one step up and dropped to her knees. "Please, Justin," she whispered.

He wouldn't tell her no this time as he had in the bedroom earlier. He wouldn't stop her. He took her hair in his hand and pulled her toward him. Her mouth was already open, her tongue sliding out and he sucked in a breath, braced himself with his other hand on the banister and waited for the first touch, that first lick, that first caress of her fingers.

And when it came, his breath whooshed out between his lips and it was all he could do to keep standing.

It was going to be a long afternoon.

Chapter Six

Ella lay with her head on Justin's lap, a glass of wine in one hand, his hand in her other as she looked up at the stars. Justin had a swing out behind his house that looked to simply be plopped down in the middle of the yard, but it was perfect really and far enough away from the house that the lights from inside or on the porch wouldn't interfere with the big Texas sky full of twinkling dots.

"I've never seen anything like it," she said, completely in awe.

"Kinda figured. It really is something."

"Something isn't even close." Looking up, she felt so small and insignificant and yet at the same time, she felt that if she just reached out a little, she could touch the sky with the tips of her fingers. She liked that idea. She liked believing she could just reach out and touch her dreams. She squeezed his hand at that thought and turned her head slightly so she could bring his face into focus.

The sky wasn't the only something she was in awe of. She repeated her statement from the night in the truck on the way to his bed. "Two days isn't enough, Justin."

He looked down at her and brushed her hair from her face. "No, it's not."

"I meant, it's not enough to know."

"It's not just been two days, baby. It's been many more days. Maybe not in physical contact and proximity, but it's been much more than two days. We're real good at two days though. I'd like to try for longer sometime soon."

He was right. Their relationship spanned much more than the days she'd spent on the ranch and there were a lot of two-day weekends they'd spent together. They did need more than that, she just didn't know if she could give it. "I don't want to have to go to New Orleans tomorrow."

"I don't want to let you go, but I have to. I'd rather keep you here, bind you to the bed so I can come home and slide right inside you. I can't do that though. You have a job you love, and I have a job I like."

She took a sip of her wine. It still saddened her, the whole regular life thing. She didn't want to leave this idyllic little world of him and sex and delicious food like the steak sandwiches he'd made her earlier and sex and sleeping in that amazing bed and sex and him. She had no idea what she was supposed to do on Saturday morning when she would normally head home to Birmingham. Was she supposed to go back to life as it had been before he had showed up on her doorstep?

When she'd left him the times before, she hadn't wanted to leave, but she'd always thought, somewhere in her mind, that she could return to him if she wanted. He never pressured her for more, never asked. But did he even need to ask? She could return to Texas and Justin whenever she wanted, right? He'd welcome her with open arms, wouldn't he?

And could it really be that simple?

"You're thinking too hard, baby."

"Yes."

"About what? Tell me."

And that inquiry, that curious concern made her ache and sigh and wish and dream and hope. He always asked, always wanted to know, always wanted to help if he could. She was important to him, and he let her know it. He never let her just assume it, he told her, asked about her, gave her his attention no matter what it was, big thoughts or small.

Did she give the same in return? Did he know how important he was to her? Another swallow of wine went down bitterly, along with her thoughts. No, he probably didn't know. She'd avoided seeing him these last couple of months and kept herself locked away emotionally most of the time. How would he know what he meant to her with all her walls up?

She was likely a damn fool.

Some liked to keep their thoughts to themselves, but after years of feeling as though her ex cared little for them, it was like a balm to her soul that Justin made it a point to ask and be interested. She only wished she could take and follow his lead and not fear the niggling little thought that she'd once again be rejected if she opened up. "Thinking about what happens after Saturday."

"What do you mean?"

"Well, the last session of my training class is over at noon and I'm supposed to fly home." She turned her head against his thighs, tried to ignore the not-so-easy-to-ignore bulge in his jeans against her cheek, and looked up at him. She smiled when she found him looking down at her, concern etched on his face in moonlight.

Yeah, she needed to be serious here and not give in to the temptation to avoid the rest of the conversation and nibble on his cock. "I don't know what to do."

"What do you want to do?"

Fuck you. Come live with you. "I don't know." Why did she find it so hard to admit the truth to him? She could open up and tell him anything and she knew that, deep down in her soul she knew that, but then there were moments that the truth scared the crap out of her and she bit her tongue to keep from letting it spill over. Besides, living with him wouldn't be a wise thing to do at this stage. Maybe not at any stage.

He nodded and lifted his free hand to again brush hair from her face. The caress was so tender it made her heart hurt.

"It's hard to do anything when you don't know what you want to do."

"What do you want me to do?"

Justin shook his head. "I can't tell you that. I got you down here. I got you out of your comfort zone to face some dirty desires. I got you some damn good sex and some pampering. But, I can't tell you what I want you to do. I don't want to influence you in that way because once the words are out there..."

"You're no help," she grumbled, knowing he was right. If she heard the words, even though she already knew what they'd be, if she heard them, she wouldn't be able to resist them.

He laughed low and sexy. But then, it seemed everything he did was low and sexy.

"So, now I'm mean *and* no help. Not very gracious of you, baby, after all I've done for you since Sunday." He *tsked* and shook his head again, this time in a very disapproving manner. "I do believe this requires some form of punishment until you decide to be grateful."

He winked, kissed the back of her hand that he held and let it go, only to reach out and pinch her nipple through yet another T-shirt that he'd let her borrow. She arched in automatic reaction, which gave him opportunity to lift the shirt

95

up and expose her body. Another thing she loved that was low and sexy... The whistle of appreciation when he got his hands or his eyes on her. He made her feel beautiful, erotic and sexy.

His work-roughened hand slid up her belly to cup one of her breasts, his thumb stroking over the nipple, keeping it erect and sensitive, keeping her back arched and her chest thrust up in offering. She loved the feel of the scrape of his skin over hers. It left her feeling even more vulnerable for reasons she wasn't sure of. She just knew she liked it more than soft, smooth hands.

The contrasts between them, more than their gender, turned her on. He was lean, slender, but strong in muscle, where she was soft and rounded. He was tall and she was a bit shorter, enough to give her a feeling of being protected in his shadow. He was pensive at times, aggressive at others, laid back and casual, whereas she was not so aggressive and a little tenser. But he was wicked smart in a real world kind of way, worked hard for everything and gave still more to his friends, and he had a strong moral compass when it came to the heart. He wanted love and wanted to give love, but knew that it took a lot more than the words to make it work. Not to mention his open-minded sexual desires, which if someone were to look too closely at, might think he had no moral center at all. She knew differently.

She was open-minded too, loved the things they'd done together, but she was a little more reserved and he delighted in breaking through those reserves. Truth be told, she delighted in the breaking in and breaking through as well.

"Ouch!" She nearly came off the swing and his lap as pain exploded through her nipple from where he was pinching.

"You drifted, and I wanted you back."

"So you pinched me hard enough to...to..." She couldn't finish the sentence as she laid her head back down and tried to get her breathing under control.

"No, sit up and scoot your ass in my lap." He still held her nipple, though very gently, and she sat and moved so she was sitting sideways in his lap. "Good girl," he whispered as he nuzzled her neck before lifting her breast in his palm and sucking the tip between his lips.

Ella moaned and melted against the arm that was braced at her back. Liquid heat slid through her body as he pulled and tugged and nibbled, soothing the previous soreness into tender, insistent pleasure. She could do little more than recline into his body and accept his touch.

Her eyes were closed when he lifted his head. The hand holding her breast drifted down to her mound, then he sank his fingers into her wet sex. There was no coaxing, no teasing, no gentle urging. He simply thrust them upward, burying them deep. She wore no underwear and no bra under his T-shirt. She hadn't needed to. She hadn't wanted to. Her outer thigh, the one closest to the edge of the swing, moved, almost of its own accord, giving him more access to her folds. His thumb, instead of rasping against her nipple, pressed and rasped against her clit. The arm at her back shifted her slightly until Justin could lower his head to her other breast, latching onto the nipple.

More pleasure spiked through her and flowed down from her chest, into her belly. His fondling was erratic, slow and steady in and out, followed by hard and heavy thrusting, then sliding from inside to rub from her clit down to her opening and back again. And she lay there, basking in the attention from his mouth and his hand, her eyes staring upward at the sky.

"Don't wander from me again, Ella," he murmured against her. "Stay with me, feel it, feel me."

But she was with him, she was just floating, or at least it felt like floating. Something about the big Texas sky and the warm air brushing her skin mixed with the very real human touch of Justin and she was there with him, only...

His fingers slid back into her, forcing her complete attention. "Look at me." His gaze clashed with hers as he pumped his hand between her legs. "What were you thinking about?"

"Nothing... I... Floating. Overwhelmed with it. So perfect."

"I'll give you overwhelmed in a bit, baby. I promise. This is nothing compared to what's coming, but just stay with me. You can float later." He kissed the tip of her nose. "Now look, watch my hand."

Slowly, as if it took a moment for the words to sink in, she turned her head and looked. His hand was moving, fingers fucking inside her, thumb flicking the end of her clit, time and again. She spread her leg wider, tried to get a better look, tried to see more for now she was lost in this, in the visual of what he was doing, not just the feel.

And then he curled his fingers up, hooked them against the front wall of her pussy and moved his thumb, pushing the heel of his hand against her clit. He rocked her like that until she started to move on her own, undulating and thrusting her hips up from his lap, gripping his knee for support.

"That's it, baby. That's it."

The Texas sky all but forgotten, she started to see stars of her own as her eyes closed and slid her own hand between her legs, curved it over the back of his and jerked herself off on his fingers.

"More, girl. Give it to me. Come for me."

"Yes," she breathed. "Yes."Louder this time. "Yes, yes, yes." Even louder. "Justin, yes," she shrieked.

He held her tight around the back as the swing bounced and swayed on its chains and she came in a flood of heat and wetness and breathless cries. She moved against the muscles in his thighs and felt the ridge of his erection at her hip.

"That's my Ella," he said softly, once again nuzzling his face into her neck.

Justin knelt in front of her. "Blindfold or not?"

Ella was kneeling naked on the floor in his living room. He'd gotten her to the back porch and stripped the shirt off her after the orgasm on the swing. He'd told her he had something planned for her. He'd wanted to do this yesterday, but hadn't had the energy after the blowjob on the stairs, followed by sex in the shower, a nap and more sex. She wore him the hell out in the most amazing ways. He wouldn't trade it for anything.

"I don't know. What are you going to do?"

"That wasn't part of my question. Yes or no?" She licked her lips and wouldn't meet his gaze. "Ella? Do you trust me?"

She looked at him then. "Yes. Of course I trust you. I just... I don't know."

"Then I won't." He leaned forward and kissed her on the forehead in what he hoped was a tender, reassuring gesture. He wasn't going to hurt her, but he wanted to pleasure her, give her something incredible to remember that he'd never tried before.

He stood and backed up a few feet, inch by inch pulling his shirt up his torso, making sure she was watching, making sure she was taking it all in. She liked ogling him, so he figured he'd indulge her. Give her the chance to look her fill.

He tugged the shirt off over his head and dropped it to the couch. He caught her licking her lips and saw her nostrils flare. She was turned on again. Still. Always. Just as he was.

Gliding his hands down his stomach, he framed his cock behind his jeans in a lewd gesture with his hands. Her eyes widened, and she swallowed hard. Her pretty nipples pebbled and if he touched them, he knew they'd be stiff against his fingers, his tongue, between his teeth. He'd bet his life's savings she was dripping wet too.

Slowly, oh so very slowly, he released one button at a time from its buttonhole. Her eyes were trained on every move of his fingers. She pulled her bottom lip between her teeth and nibbled as she watched. So focused on him, he imagined she'd forgotten she was naked. He didn't think she cared though. Naked didn't seem to bother her with him, something he was exceedingly glad about because he loved seeing her bare body.

"Ella?" She didn't look up or make any move like she'd heard him. "Ella?"

"Huh?"

She still hadn't removed her stare from his crotch. "Ella, look up at me." It took a few seconds for her to comply but eventually she did, her gaze leaving a heated trail up to his face. "Good girl. Now keep your eyes on mine."

She shook her head and looked back down at his jeans where the denim was parted over his hard cock. The damn thing was threatening to spill out for her viewing pleasure, but he wasn't ready for that. "B-but, Justin..."

She pouted as she locked stares with him, but the hunger was still there. She was fighting hard to do as he'd said, but the struggle was rough. He loosened another button, and she fisted her hands against her thighs. Another button and she bit down hard on her lip. The last button and she whimpered, her eyes full of disappointment.

Justin freed his cock to the cool air of the room and still she kept her gaze on his. He walked toward her and watched as her head tilted back to keep from looking at anything other than his face. She blinked when he stood within inches, close enough that he'd have to tug her head backward slightly to get his cock between her lips, but that's exactly what he intended to do.

"Don't look away from me and open your mouth."

Eagerly she complied. He'd never seen her mouth open so wide so quickly, but the second it was open and his hand was in her hair, he slid his cock over her tongue and deep into her throat. She gagged and he pulled out, only to do it again. She was able to take him now that she knew what he was planning. She started to raise her hands, and he shook his head. She dropped them back to her thighs. "Just your mouth, baby. Open that pretty throat for me."

She closed her mouth, swallowed, and then opened to him again. She stuck her tongue out, and he glided over it and down. She huffed out a breath through her nose and for a moment, he saw panic in her eyes, but soon it died out.

She was beautiful this way. Hell, she was beautiful any way, but he didn't know a man alive who didn't like a woman on her knees with his dick in her mouth. With his free hand, he held the base steady and continued to guide it in and out of the wet cavern. "Such a good girl."

And she smiled up at him with her eyes. There was happiness in the green orbs even though he couldn't see as much of the green as he had before this little teasing session began. He extended his leg a little and nudged at her knees. "Spread your legs for me."

As soon as she shifted and spread for him, he stepped a little closer, slid his cock down her throat a little deeper and held her stare a little longer. No movement, hardly a breath coming from him, just a ton of feeling, both physical and emotional. He could've stayed like that for hours, just looking into her eyes, feeling her throat working around his cock, feeling the soft tug on the head, but he couldn't. She needed to breathe.

He smiled at her and slipped his cock from her mouth then bent to kiss her. Her lips and tongue attacked him as soon as he was within range, the lust and hunger bubbling to the surface and he held her head steady and took everything she had to give.

He knelt in front of her with only minor difficulty, given his hardness. "You're such a good girl for me, Ella," he whispered when the kiss broke.

"I try," she whispered back.

"Why don't we see how naughty you can be for me now?" With his hand still fisted in her hair, he shifted to the side. From under the couch, he pulled out a length of rope and a Hitachi wand. Only once before had he used one on a woman, and she'd just about climbed the walls. It had freaked them both out, but he soon learned it was from intense orgasms and sensations rather than any sort of fear of the device. He kissed Ella's shoulder and stood. "Lift your arms over your head."

She did it, and he gripped her wrists in one hand and began working the rope with the other, winding it around each wrist, twisting it and winding it around the other wrist. He tugged and was happy with the strength. "Is it too tight?"

Ella flexed her fingers, rotated her wrists. "No."

He pulled up hard on the length he held in his hand. "How about now?"

She shook her head, letting go a moan of pleasure. "No."

He loved her responsiveness, her openness, her trust in this, in him with this. "Good." He wrapped the rope again, this time around both wrists, and then threaded it up from the bottom, looping it into a knot, which he secured with yet another knot. He slid his fingers through the loops and pulled upward again. "Now?"

She hissed for him. "No."

"Too loose?"

"No."

"Good. Lift up on your knees." When she was in position, he tugged her arms a little straighter and hooked the rope thought a clip, which was secured to the end of another length of rope he'd flipped over one of the exposed beams crossing the ceiling. "Pull down now."

He watched her pull, twist and tug and the rope didn't give one way or the other. He grinned. "Good. You feel okay?"

"A little nervous." She looked up, her face screwed up in confusion. "When did you do that?"

Justin laughed. "After you went out to the swing. I thought for sure you'd have noticed it when we came back inside."

"I clearly wasn't paying attention."

"Clearly. Ready to play?"

Her gaze found his, full of hope and anticipation, a giddy excitement. "Do I get to suck your cock again?"

"Nope." For a moment she looked crushed, saddened, but then...

"Sex?"

"Not yet." She eyed him up and down, her brow furrowed in thought and confusion. He liked the moments she couldn't figure out what he was up to.

He knelt beside her again and smoothed her hair where his fingers had been embedded before. Leaning over, he licked at one distended nipple and she arched, thrusting her chest forward. He took it as an invitation and suckled more of her breast into his mouth.

After a few moments, he moved across her chest to her other breast. This one he nipped at, biting gently at the tip before laving it with long, slow licks of his tongue.

She twisted in the rope, doing her best to offer more of herself to him and he smiled against her skin, enjoying her insatiable need for sex, for pleasure, for him, for what he could do to her and for her. He never touched her pussy, not as he knew she wanted, but lowering his head, he could smell her arousal, her hunger. The musk was strong, and even from his angle, he could see the glistening wetness on her cunt lips. She was ready.

Justin trailed his fingers up the inside of her left thigh and down the inside of her right one. She shivered. He did it again, this time pausing to stoke the crease between her leg and her pussy. Her breath hitched, and she thrust her hips forward.

"Please, Justin."

"I promise to." He kissed her belly, and then sat up. "Do you remember a trivia question either the first night or the second that I joined your group that the answer was Hibachi but someone said Hitachi wand? And the subsequent conversation at the table about sex toys?"

Ella laughed and nodded. "Sex toy talk with half the table sober and the other half drunk on beer..." She shook her head then. "That was interesting."

Justin laughed at the memory as well. There had been an incredible amount of obscene language, hand gestures and comparing of toys, with the women, including Ella, opting for the pleasure of the Rabbit toy over a normal, everyday vibrator or dildo. However, none had ever tried the Hitachi wand. "Yes, it was. Which brings me to our activity tonight."

He held up the wand, and her eyes grew wide. Again, he read anticipation, but there was nervousness, uncertainty.

"I-I've never used one, Justin." She licked her lips, and her gaze traveled from one end of the toy to the other.

"I know. I thought your first time would be better if we were both around to witness it. And with you being tied up..." He left the sentence dangling in the air between them. He didn't say anything further and neither did she as he gave her time to look her fill of the wand.

"Have you turned it on before?" she asked, her bottom lip once again being worried between her teeth.

"Yes. It's quite powerful. It can be used as more than a sex toy. Very good as a massager I'm told. Here, let's see what you think."

He waited for her consent, just a nod of her head, before he turned it on to the low setting. He tried not to smile when she jolted a little at the loud buzzing. Slowly he lifted the head of the wand to the back of her shoulder. She immediately dropped her head forward and moaned.

Running it back and forth over her muscles, he watched as she continued to relax. Her arms lost their tension, and her entire body sagged as much as it could with her wrists bound above her head. Her legs widened and once more she moaned in pleasure. He could only imagine what would happen once he pressed it against her clit.

It was about time to find out.

He switched it off and she simply knelt there, hunched forward. "Are you okay?"

"Mm-hmm. Very much so."

"You liked it then?"

"Loved it."

He petted her hair. "Good. Ready to see how much more you can love it?" He fisted his hand in the soft strands and tugged her head up.

"Oh yes."

Heat filled her eyes as she looked up at him. He bent his head and licked her lower lip, unable to resist a taste of her lush mouth. While he savored and tangled his tongue with hers, he turned the toy on again, still on low and touched it to the top of her thigh.

She started in his hold but soon relaxed, giving in to it.

Lifting his head a scant inch from hers, he watched her eyes as he moved the wand up her body. They darkened, widened, pleaded with him the closer he got to her breasts. Touching her nipple for less than a heartbeat, she attempted to buckle forward. "Too much?" he whispered.

"N-no. More."

He touched her nipple with the end of the wand again, this time for a bit longer. She jolted but kept her gaze focused on him. Her pupils dilated beautifully, and her breathing became harsher the longer he teased her breast. He moved the toy in a circle under and around her nipple, along the outer edges of her areola, and only when she was whimpering and seeming to gasp for breath did he move to the other breast and give it the same deliberate attention.

"Justin, please."

He could just see the beginning of tears forming in her eyes. She'd always been responsive to touch, to teasing stimulation of tongue and fingers, but he'd never seen her like this. This was a whole new level for her, for them. He liked it. He liked it a lot.

Taking the toy from her body but leaving it buzzing, he gave her a chance to calm, to catch her breath again, but not for long. He still wanted her on that edge of need because he wanted her to fall over, give over to it, completely lose herself in bliss. He didn't know if she ever had, not with him, not with anyone, but he wanted to get her there and take her over.

He kissed her mouth once, twice, three times and on the fourth, just as he slid his tongue between her parted lips, he brought the wand back to her body, this time though between her legs. She cried out in his mouth as her body bucked. She was coming. Already she was coming.

He pulled back from the too short kiss to look into her face. He saw shock in her eyes. "Ella? Are you okay, baby?" She nodded. At least he thought she nodded. She made a jerky up-and-down movement with her head that mimicked a nod. He loosened his grip on the wand and started to pull it away from her, but she shook her head.

"No. More. Please. More."

"You want more?"

"Y-yes. H-harder."

"Okay." And so he gave it to her harder. He pushed the wand tight against her clit and turned it on high. Ella screamed as another orgasm shook her. She swayed in her bonds, on her knees. Her nipples were harder and tighter than he'd ever seen them and the urge to draw one into his mouth was strong, but not as strong as the desire to continue watching her face.

He turned the wand back to low and he could see in her eyes a bit of calm, like that before a storm rages. She wasn't done, her body wasn't finished. "More, Ella?"

"M-more," she whispered. "Please," she said without a sound, just the word forming heavily on her lips.

Justin turned the wand on high again. She pulled on the rope above her and while he thought she might be trying to get away from the intensity the toy must be providing to such a sensitive area, he quickly realized she was trying to hold on, trying to hold herself together before she blew apart once more.

"Let it go, baby."

Chapter Seven

"Let it go, baby."

Justin's voice was a faraway beacon, the anchor she clung to, even more than she clung to the rope above her head. Another orgasm was threatening to shatter her and she was right there waiting, willing, wanting. She'd never felt anything like it. Her entire body was nothing but a road map of imaginary pinpricks. She tingled all over and the trembling of her thigh muscles, the fluttering in her belly was unlike any other trembling or flutterings she'd experienced.

The wand. Love. Hate. Good. Evil. Pain. Pleasure. It was all mixed into that one device, and what he didn't understand was that she had no control over giving more or letting go. The wand simply took everything from her, forced her body to give up the orgasm. And she wanted it that way. Needed it.

Then it was there, taking her over, pulling the wetness from inside her, pulling whole body sensations from her until she was screaming, crying, begging incoherently for it to stop, for it to go on forever.

Her belly clenched and her upper body swayed while her lower body tensed and pushed down on the wand, trying to wring every bit of pleasure it could from the toy.

"God," she groaned. "Justin." Another orgasm followed and still another. Darkness edged her vision. Come coated her thighs. She couldn't take anymore. It was unbearable, the pleasure so intense it bordered on the most incredible pain where the two mixed and became one.

She twisted, trying to get away from it, and then it was gone, the room silent save for her shivering sobs, and Justin was there. He was everything solid and real and he was there, wrapping her up in his arms, the front of his body pressed against the back of hers. Her head fell back against his shoulder and tremors still racking her body, her pussy still constricting upon itself, the muscles still rippling with aftershocks of her multiple releases.

Justin stroked her arms and down her sides until her breathing calmed and her tears stopped. She wasn't crying crying, she was simply so overcome, so wrung out that she had no control over her body.

He stood and pressed his legs to her back, giving her something to brace herself against while he unhooked the rope then began to unwind it from her wrists. "You're going to ache, and you're going to hurt until all the blood starts flowing properly again."

The rope landed on the floor beside her and he knelt again behind her, massaging her arms before slowly helping her to lower them. She winced at the pain and sank down to the floor, her ass resting against her calves. He hadn't been joking about the pain and aches.

"Your legs are going to ache and hurt too."

She nodded. They already did. She wouldn't have traded the pleasure and the orgasms for all the comfort in the world though. "I know. I'll have to crawl around for a while before I can stand and walk, I think."

"Mmmm." He pressed his mouth to the side of her neck. "I might like the idea of you crawling around naked."

"Might, my ass. You'd love it, but this floor isn't good for crawling. Too hard on a girl's knees."

He laughed and nipped at her shoulder. "Good to see you haven't lost your sense of humor and sarcasm. If I thought there was a chance at having you on all fours more than once in a great blue moon, I'd get the whole place carpeted."

"Nice, plush carpeting?"

"Only the very best for my pet."

Ella scoffed at the word pet. "Woof."

He swatted her outer thigh. "Brat."

She moaned. She didn't think her body would welcome any further sensations, any further play or teasing or touch even, but she moaned when he spanked her. She quickly bit her lip, wondering if he'd take her noise as an invitation to do it again. She wasn't sure she wanted it, but at the same time...

"Ella?"

His hand rubbed the spot he'd slapped, and she suddenly wanted more. "Spank me, Justin."

"You sure?"

She heard the excitement he couldn't contain. "Yes."

"Then give me your ass, and I'll oblige you."

It was impossible for her pussy to clench and ooze happiness at his tone, at his words, but it sure did. Slowly she leaned forward and winced at the stiffness in her hips and knees. On all fours, she was trembling in both need and exhaustion, but she wanted this, she wanted to feel his hands on her. She'd be leaving tomorrow and wouldn't see him again for either days or months. She needed this from him, the smarting she knew she'd feel until the end of the week. Provided he didn't hold back as she knew he might.

"Drop to your elbows if you need to. I know your arms have to be burning."

Relief she didn't know she'd been harboring flowed through her. She did as he'd suggested and sighed, taking the weight off her wrists and shoulders. Much better.

Rough hands caressed the tender skin of her behind.

Then, rough hands spanked the tender skin of her behind. First one cheek by one hand followed by the next cheek with the other hand. Then one hand braced at the small of her back and a succession of echoing pops landed dead center of each cheek. One right after the other. Justin didn't give her a chance to breathe between them. He didn't give her a chance to protest or praise. He simply let loose on her, and she simply reveled in it.

He knew what she wanted or needed at any given time, sometimes before she did, sometimes because she didn't. He watched her, listened to her, touched her. He gave her his full and complete attention and he knew her.

And then there was a rip and tear of foil, a swearing and he was inside her, thrusting hard up into her pussy, fucking, taking, still spanking her ass. Her body, her mind, her heart all were in overload. She wouldn't be able to come again if her life depended on it and she could barely move from the weak, jellylike state of her muscles, but she'd be damned if he wasn't going to get a good ride out of it.

She wiggled her ass against him and one smack later, he gripped her hips and pulled her into him. "You want to play like that, do you?"

She wiggled her ass again, only to find herself grabbed and squeezed, the tenderness from the spanking smarting and causing her to hiss out a breath. "Yeah. I want to play like that."

"Good girl. Let's go."

Holding her hip in one hand, Justin reached up and held on to her shoulder, his fingers digging into her flesh. He pulled and pushed all at the same time, using her as resistance to his thrust. There was no movement from her as he held her fast in his hands against his body.

She tried to press backward, but his hand clutched hard on her hip. She tried to arch her back, but his fingers tightened on her shoulder. His hips and cock and balls slammed into her, fast paced and breathless.

He grunted behind her, whispered her name in urgency, picked up speed and groaned, going still almost immediately.

He stiffened and tensed, his fingers flexing against her skin and then he was surrounding her, his arms wrapping under her body, his chest flat against her back. Ragged, heavy breathing flipped the ends of her hair around as he lay there, calming.

"Damn, baby. I don't think I can walk now."

Ella smiled and closed her eyes. "We can crawl together."

"Speak for yourself. I'm just gonna stay right here. You make a nice pillow."

She laughed. "Ass."

"Oh yes, baby, you have a lovely warm one now. It'll be bright pink for a little while and will likely sting some tomorrow. You'll be squirming all the way to New Orleans."

"That's not the only thing that will be smarting tomorrow. I think you fucked me raw, and combined with the orgasms... I've never had multiples before."

Justin kissed her shoulder and lifted his hips up, pulling his cock out of her pussy. She felt the loss travel up her body and wanted to cry. She was going to miss him.

"There's gonna be a lot of multiples in our future, baby."

He sounded so sure of himself, of them. "I better learn how to handle them then," was all she could say.

"Yep. Now, about that crawling thing. Can you make it up the stairs or do you need me to start the shower down here?"

No way could she make it up the stairs at the moment, and hell, she wasn't sure she'd be able to make it up the stairs after a shower, but... "Down here. Then you can do your caveman thing and throw me over your shoulder and carry me upstairs."

"Bossy."

"Yep."

He kissed the top of her head when he walked around in front of her. She watched him cross the floor to the guest bath, his jeans hanging off his ass, his hair in disarray. He was the sexiest man she'd ever known and she sure as shit hoped she'd make the right decision when the time came.

The shower turned on. Crap. "Guess I have to move now," she muttered. Slowly, she raised herself, screwing up her face at the pain in her arms and shoulders. It would be a miracle if she made it across the open living room to the bathroom. Then Justin stepped out and leaned against the doorjamb, crooked his finger at her and smiled.

"Come to me, baby."

Justin turned at the traffic light, following the signs leading to Dallas-Fort Worth International Airport. "What's your training class on?"

Ella sipped on the small caramel macchiato and sighed in bliss. "It's a new property in the French Quarter that we've just acquired. It's a beautiful place with a lot of character, draws a moderate business crowd but most of their business is tourist traffic on weekends. Their front office staff needs to be trained on how to deal with the different types of guests. Before we took over, they didn't get a lot of business people."

She leaned forward and tried not to wince as she put the cardboard cup in the cup holder. She tried not to sigh as she sat back. Last night's play was quite evident across her body, both inside and out. Marks from Justin's fingers were on her shoulder and her hip, blurred handprints were tattooed on her behind. He hadn't been kidding when he said she would be having a hard time sitting. She tried not to squirm because she knew there was no comfortable sitting position, then tore off a piece of the sweet pastry in her lap.

"And you enjoy this new position? Traveling and the new responsibilities?"

She nodded, fully enjoying the way the buttery concoction melted on her tongue before swallowing. "Oh yes. I love it. This is the most travel I've ever done and so seeing the new places has been amazing, learning how different parts of the country work. It helps that I really do love the company. Corporate truly does care about their hotels and their employees and of course their guests."

"And your job is to train a lot of the front people?"

"Yes, which is completely nerve-racking for me sometimes because I'm just not good in front of a group of people, but I know my job and I know this hotel's policies like the back of my hand. I know what they want and I—"

"You're comfortable in your knowledge, in your expertise." Statement, not question.

She nodded excitedly. "Exactly." The more she talked about work, the more she smiled, the more it lessened the ache that came with the fact he would leave her at the airport for her flight to New Orleans and he would go back home.

Home. It wasn't her home, but he'd made her feel as though it were, as though it could be. He gave her free reign and let her move about comfortably.

"I'm proud of you. You've come out of your shell some and you're becoming this woman who—"

"I didn't think I could be," she finished for him.

"Yeah, that."

"I know. A lot of things changed in a relatively short period of time." She knew that was part of why she tried not to get attached to him. Okay that wasn't exactly true. From the word Go, she'd been attached to him. It didn't go away just because she pulled back to get some things in line and to figure out what it was she wanted to do about him, how she wanted him to fit into her life and how she wanted to fit into his. She didn't want him to just be some guy she had a few weekend flings with and she knew he was so much more than that, had been so much more than that for a long time, even if she hadn't wanted to admit it before.

She picked at her pastry some more, looking out the window without really seeing anything and mewled when he took hold of her hair and gave it a light tug. She'd promised herself she wasn't going to cry today, but damn, if the tears weren't threatening. She couldn't be in such an emotional state only to walk away from him and do the job she had to do. Then again, throwing herself into her work for the next few days would be a good thing. She wouldn't have time to think and dwell on Justin until night came and she was alone in her room.

"You all right, baby?"

"Yeah, just…" She shook her head, unsure how to put into words what she was thinking, what she was wondering and feeling.

"I'm not going anywhere, Ella. No matter how far away you have to go to find your way back, I'm not going anywhere. I'll be right here, waiting."

She knew that. Hearing him say it, just like hearing him not say other things last night out on the swing... It was all real, sometimes more so with words and other times with actions or even silence. He wasn't going anywhere, at least not unless she told him to go away, and she couldn't ever imagine doing that. She just had to figure out how to ask him to keep her.

"I'd have driven you all the way to New Orleans too."

"I know. It's better this way."

His hand tightened in her hair. "How do you figure that?"

She slanted him a look. "If you'd taken me to the hotel, you would have been tempted to come in and try out the bed in my room."

He barked out a laugh. "Shit, woman. As if you could keep your hands off me when there's a bed or not in proximity."

"I don't know what you're talking about. I've been a perfect lady with you."

"You keep telling yourself that, but we both know it's bullshit."

It was her turn to laugh. Okay, yeah, it was bullshit. She'd been way too eager not to be a lady. Maybe a lady slut, but there were moments where the lady part of it clearly was kicked out of the equation. He had the utmost respect for her, but down on her knees, come dripping down her thighs, her arms stretched over her head, and orgasm upon orgasm reducing her to nothing more than a quivery puddle of goo... Lady didn't come into the same universe and she'd take that state of being any day of the week over being a proper anything. Well, anything other than being properly his.

She loved that he could tease her out her maudlin thoughts, her too serious thoughts. It wasn't that he didn't want her to ever be serious, he just liked when she laughed and smiled. He wanted to help, to fix things, and he couldn't do it all. Some things she had to work out on her own. Until he got impatient and took matters into his own hands or took her into his own hands.

"You're thinking about it again, aren't you?"

"What?"

"Don't what me. You're thinking about sex again."

"I am not."

"Again. Bullshit. I see it in the blush on your cheeks and how you keep looking out the corner of your eye at me. Your nipples are pebbled against that shirt and bra, and I bet if I reached between your legs, I'd find your panties soaking wet."

"You don't know what you're talking about," she huffed. She was lying, too. They both knew he was dead-on with his assessment. She *was* thinking about sex with him again. She was thinking about him naked and hard and inside her.

There were three things in her life that gave her purpose and made her feel alive. Him, sex with him, and her job. Probably in that order too.

She loved her friends and her family, but her job was something that was all hers. Then there was Justin. She loved him, as well. He was all hers if she was willing to give it a shot.

Love.

Him.

Just as that realization dawned, she saw the signs for the airport. Tempered with her elation at finally admitting it to herself, there was the trepidation of leaving him, of not knowing how to or what to do next.

"Do you want me to park and go in with you or...?"

"I think I love you, Justin." She clapped a hand over her mouth. She couldn't believe she just blurted it out like that. She knew it was more than an 'I think' too. But did she have to just throw it out like that?

He switched lanes immediately. "Parking it is. Terminal?"

She chanced a glance in his direction. The smile on his face warmed her and worked to steady the frantic beating of her heart, but with the words out there, she couldn't help but feel a little...or rather a lot nervous. "Huh?"

"What gate are you leaving out of? What terminal do we need to park at? There's parking for each one."

"Oh. Right. Ummm," she dug in the side pocket of her purse for her boarding pass. "E. Terminal E."

"Got it.

Justin pulled into the parking garage, took a ticket and put it up on the dash. Ella watched him closely for any sign of how he was feeling about what she'd said, but his facial expression never changed as he made his way through the dark and very crowded aisles of the garage.

"Justin?" She was confused when he passed a few empty parking spaces on the terminal side.

"Yeah?" He took another ramp up to the next level and crept along until he found a corner spot at the very far end. It was dark, surrounded by other cars and he backed in neatly. He turned the engine off, unbuckled his seatbelt and pressed the button that would move the driver's seat backward. That was when he looked at her. Finally, looked at her. "What time is your flight?"

She looked down at her boarding pass. "In an hour and a half."

"Okay, so we got a few minutes."

"For what? Justin, are we okay? I mean... What I said was...."

He reached over and depressed her seatbelt latch, put her purse on the floor at her feet and took her hand. "Climb over here," he said, unzipping his jeans and pulling his cock out.

He was rock hard, the head poking just a bit outside the foreskin. He stroked it slowly, watching her, his eyes a stormy gray-green, and for the life of her she couldn't tell what he was thinking or feeling. Well, other than the fact he was aroused, but that wasn't anything new.

He motioned for her. "C'mon, Ella. Crawl over to me. You know you want to."

She damn sure did. Whatever her admission to loving him meant to him, it didn't diminish his desire or lust for her. That was a good sign, right?

What was left of the pastry went back into its bag and up on the dash. She turned in her seat and leaned forward toward him, pulled one leg up on the cushion and worked her way over the center console. He helped her straddle his thighs, and with hands on her waist, lowered her slightly until the head of his cock rubbed against the soaking wet crotch of her panties.

A smile crossed his lips. "Told you I'd find you wet."

Ella did nothing more than nod. No use denying it or trying to defend it. It was just what he did to her, the effect he had on her body. She wasn't ashamed of it and even reveled in it. No one had ever made her feel this beautiful, this sexy just by the way he looked at her and knew her body, sometimes better than she knew it. "Condom?"

He nodded and pulled her close for a kiss, sweet and slow, just a meeting and melding of lips. But the second his tongue reached out, his hand was in her hair, grasping and tugging, holding her prisoner against him, willing though she may be.

Her fists gripped his shirt, her hips moved, sliding her silky panties over his cock head. The kiss deepened and mutual moans of pleasure echoed around the interior of the truck. He pulled her head back and leaned forward to bite her chin. She thrust her hips toward him and sank down, little by little. His cock pushed against her panties, pushed them inside her. She lifted and lowered herself again.

"Naughty girl. You keep that up and I'm going to come on those panties."

Ella moaned. She didn't care. She wanted him to. She wanted him to come on her, in her, because of her, about her. Her skirt slid up her legs and she wrapped her hands around his head, laying her cheek against his hair and fucked his cock head with her panties still covering her pussy.

"Shit, baby."

Justin reached between their bodies and as she lifted, he pulled her panties to the side and pushed himself up inside her. His hands grabbed her ass, and he fucked her.

It wasn't soft and tender and loving. And she didn't care. She never cared with him. She liked it hard and fast and rough. She liked when he would lose control and take her, take what he wanted from her body.

"Condom, Justin," she said softly into the heated truck.

"No, I know. Baby, I know." He just kept fucking her, bouncing her on his cock, on his lap, his hands hitting his thighs when she'd slide down.

Their first time without a condom was in his truck. Ella might have laughed if she'd had the breath for it. As it was, her breathing was labored, her skin slick with sweat, her eyes fogged and unfocused. She was riding him in the parking garage of the Dallas/Fort Worth International Airport, and for that moment, she didn't care that he didn't wear a condom. She only wanted the slide of his cock inside her, hard up inside her. She was the only woman he'd been with for the last year, and he was the only man she'd been with in longer than that as she and her ex hadn't been sexually active for the last few years of their marriage.

She worked one hand between them much as he had when he pushed her panties out of the way. She reached for her clit, lifted up on her knees a little more, which made him lift higher too. She pressed her pelvis against his belly and ground her finger onto her clit, rocking her hips, taking the control of the fuck long enough to...

"Oh God, Justin," she panted. "Oh God, oh shit."

He reached up and wrapped his hands around her shoulders from behind and provided some resistance to her lifting. He was holding her down in the only way he could from their position, and she lost it. He gave her the fuck but held onto the control of her.

The orgasm drenched them both and in one smooth motion, he lifted her and pulled out of her. "Put your panties in place," he said, his gaze transfixed between her legs.

Shaking, Ella pulled her hand from her panties and righted the material, screen-printed with cupcakes. Her body still squeezed on the inside, her eyes were unfocused and her heart threatened to beat right out of her chest.

He angled her hips forward with an arm around her ass. "Lean back and hold that position right there. Careful not to push the horn." He winked.

With his other hand, he jacked off. He pushed against her panties again and stroked his cock in his fist. She stared down at the masturbation scene before her, stared at his hand moving up and down on the shaft, sliding the foreskin back and forth over the tip. His hips were lifting, and she raised her arms above her head and pushed into the roof of the truck.

His breathing was labored and his eyes were narrowed. Their gazes locked and stayed that way, even as he started to come, the force of the sperm from his cock shooting sensation against her clit where the head was separated from it by her panties.

He grunted through his orgasm and his body jerked slightly, and then stiffened until the last of the semen left him. He sighed heavily and leaned his head against his seat. His gaze was on her as hers was on him. He began rubbing his come into her panties, some into her thighs, more under the waistband of her panties.

"You're going to smell like me. I love that you're going to smell like me."

"Justin," she said. "People will smell sex on me, yes. I should change panties." It was a token protest at best. They both knew if he wanted her to smell like sex, then she would smell like sex. It was becoming more and more apparent to her that she wanted to play his little games. She was fucking him in a parking garage in broad daylight. Anyone could have seen them. Anyone could have called the cops. Hell, security could have happened upon them. In the heat of the moment, she hadn't cared. Kind of like when they had left Birmingham. Taking off her panties in the parking lot. Opening her shirt so her bra could be seen. Oral sex at the rest area. Flashing her ass to the truckers.

Justin liked exposing her where they might or might not get caught. The thing that made it okay, made it better, made her want it more was that he was willing to expose himself too. He would stand by her, stick with her and take the brunt of anything if someone caught them.

He was slowly, or rather not so slowly, showing her the risk of being vulnerable. The pleasure of such was high if she trusted him, and his protection of her was worth everything.

"I want them to smell sex on you. I want them to smell *me* on you."

"It'll single me out. I don't like that."

"Why not?"

"Because you won't be with me." That was the crux of the matter. She was helpless and hopeless in the best of ways when it came to him, especially when he was with her, but when he wasn't, when she was on her own, she was shy, uncertain in most things save her job. Divorce had been a big personal chance she had taken on her own and she'd made a life by herself, but she honestly didn't want to live alone or exist alone. Sure she had friends, but what she really wanted was a lover, a man to share life with. She'd had a man, but not a lover and well, hell, she needed and craved and hungered for the lover part of the equation. It was as important as talking and communicating. At least to her. She'd lived enough years with just talking and no real communication, no intimacy or physical affection that being lonely had been inevitable.

She didn't want that again. She didn't want to be alone. She'd learned she could do it—she just didn't want to. She didn't want the dating scene either. Her single friends from work had enough horror stories about trying to date that Ella didn't want to venture into those waters.

She wanted Justin.

"I'm always with you, baby. Every word I've ever said to you is either inside your head or just a push of an app button away in your email."

124

And that was true. "But you won't be there holding my hand or there for me to hide my face against."

"Why would you want to hide? Hell baby, you know how many people would be envious of what we've been doing the last two days?"

She didn't know, but she could remember when she had been envious of people who had that same kind of wild and crazy sex life. If anyone had told her a year ago that she'd be sitting in the lap of a twenty-nine-year-old bartender-fireman in an airport parking garage having sex, she'd have told them they were just shy of admittance to the nut house.

Yet here she was.

If anyone had told her a year ago that she'd be divorced and *free* to be having sex in the lap of a twenty-nine-year-old bartender-fireman, she'd have told them they were a few watts short of a light bulb. She'd have immediately hoped for and wanted it, but she wouldn't have believed it possible, wouldn't have believed herself fed up enough with mediocre and status quo.

Yet there she was.

"I need to go," she said.

"I don't think so, Ella."

"Justin, the time." She looked at her watch. "I—"

"Not that."

"Then what?"

His hands gripped the hair that framed her face. He twisted his fingers in the strands and held her head immobile, his gaze intense and dark, mesmerizing. She was once again amazed at the many different facets of her cowboy's personality. "I don't *think* I love you. I don't *think* you think you love me either. I *know* I love you. I've known for a long-ass time that I loved you, and we've both known you love me too."

"Justin, I—"

"You're just scared to say it without qualification or justification and that's okay. You'll get there."

"It wasn't supposed to be like this," she said, leaning her forehead against his.

"It was supposed to be exactly like this," he said, trying to reassure her. "Now, you're right. You do need to go. I don't want you to miss your flight. Your job is important to you, and that makes it important to me."

"What about after, though?" The worried tone was back in her voice.

"You'll know what to do, and whatever you decide, I'll be here to support you."

At first, she wasn't sure they were talking about the same thing, but as she stared at those eyes, crystal clear but for the love shining back at her, she realized they were talking about the exact same thing. He was leaving it up to her, the direction or not, of their relationship.

She nodded, and he kissed the tip of her nose before opening his door and helping her down from his lap to the ground. She leaned against the inside of the door and adjusted her skirt and did her best on the wrinkles in her top. She might need to make a few shopping stops once she got to New Orleans. She turned to him in time to see him adjusting his jeans. She hated to see his cock put away. He was gorgeous enough that he should walk around naked all the time.

She giggled at her lusty thoughts. Must be the after-hot-sex-in-the-truck giggles.

He handed her her purse and reached back behind the seats for her laptop and carry-on bag and handed both of those to her as well. "You ready?" He got out of the truck, grabbed her suitcase, and shut the door, locking it behind him.

"Yeah." She wasn't really. She didn't want to leave him, but at the same time, she needed to get away from him. When he was near, it played tricks on her mind and all she wanted was him, day and night, night and day. She needed a break, her body needed a break, her head needed a break, but damn... Leaving him again was hard. Leaving him again without knowing what was going to happen next was hard.

She took one step and another and had just started to take another when a gust of wind blew through the garage. The scent of sex coming from her was stronger than she'd imagined it would be. It was as though he held his come-coated fingers right beneath her nose.

Heat crept up her neck and into her cheeks. She dared a look up at him, and the grin on his face told her that he'd caught a whiff of it too. Damn.

He took her hand. "C'mon, baby. I don't want anything to delay you coming back to me."

She didn't budge when he tugged. He turned to her with a raised brow. The challenge was there in his green eyes, and she hoped there was challenge staring back at him from hers. "Coming *back* to you? I thought you said it was my decision where we went from here?"

"It is your decision."

"Then why did you assume I'd be coming back to you?"

He tugged and she started walking, her hand firmly clasped in his and though she might be a bit irritated at him, she didn't want him to let go of her. Not by a long shot. Instead though, for good measure, she huffed out an irritated sigh.

"I wasn't assuming anything."

"You said coming back to you. Assuming that that's what I will decide." Why in the hell was she fighting him so hard on this? She needed to get her head on straight. Coming back to him was all she did want.

"No. Not an assumption." His voice was steady with confidence.

"Then what?"

"Hmmm." He shrugged. "Call it a prediction or a premonition. Call it a feeling in my gut that you will. Call it hope. Call it planting the seed in your head that I want you here with me in no uncertain terms."

Ella nodded and continued walking with him toward the terminal. Her body, her mind, her heart were already missing him. Not a good sign for clear thinking.

Chapter Eight

Justin fell into bed. He hadn't even bothered to take his shoes off. He landed face first and diagonal across the mattress. It was damn good to be home.

Three days and three nights of work. He was only a volunteer firefighter, but he worked his ass off around the firehouse with only a few hours' sleep a day. They'd had two emergency calls two nights in a row. One small house fire, which started because of grease and oil in the kitchen. Luckily no one was injured. It just so happened that there were surprise inspections earlier this morning at the station house too. No one had told him, but then again, that would have negated the surprise part.

Now he was just dead tired. He'd cleaned both fire engines from top to bottom. He hadn't been with the department for long, only about nine months. He did a lot of the grunt work. While there were a couple of other volunteers and even paid firemen who complained about the cleaning, scrubbing, swabbing, drills and cooking, he didn't care. He liked the hard work. It kept his body in shape and it kept his mind busy, even if it did wander more than once to Ella.

Ella.

His truck still smelled like her, like the sex they'd had at the airport. His bed still smelled like her too. He took a deep breath and buried his face in the pillow she'd used. He hadn't been back in the bed since the morning he took her to the airport. He'd loved on her body then, using his hands and his mouth to drive her up one peak and down the other. Her taste stayed with him for hours afterward and his fingertips still tingled whenever he thought about drifting them over her nipples or sliding them deep inside her.

He pulled the pillow tighter, wrapped his arms around the soft cotton and sighed deeply. She hadn't returned any of his text messages except to say hi and that she'd landed safe. He'd texted her goodnights and good mornings and love yous, but she'd not said anything.

He'd wanted to call on the few occasions he'd had a moment but hadn't. He knew she needed some space, though from what, he wasn't really sure. She either wanted to give them a try or she didn't. She was scared of something, and he wasn't sure what that something was. He just wanted her to give him a chance to alleviate those fears and settle her down against him.

He wanted her to know she could count on him to care, to give a shit, to keep asking how she was doing, how her day was, if she'd like to come on his fingers, his tongue or his cock.

He wanted to sleep with her, shower with her, eat with her. He wanted to take her up to the bar on trivia night. After his weekly games with her and their friends, he'd come back home and started a night just like it at his own bar. It was a riot, a lot of fun, and he wanted to share that with her. God, he missed those times, those nights that they would laugh until one in the morning, drink beer and get some answers right but most answers wrong.

He wanted to play with her, laugh with her, tease her. He wanted to see the damn bunny slippers beside the bed, and he wanted to fill soup bowls with the coffee she loved and craved so much.

And God, how he missed her gaze on him, that lust on her pretty face, those lips slack with hunger as she looked at him every time he turned around.

He just fucking missed her, and not knowing what in the hell she was thinking was driving him nuts. Again. Tired as he was, he wanted to get in his truck and take himself to the airport, get on a plane and knock on her hotel room door. He wanted to demand an answer from her. He wanted to threaten her with rope and tease her until she said yes. Again. As always, he just wanted her.

"Fuck."

Rolling over, he sat up and tugged his boots off. His whole body ached. He'd taken a bit of a nap at the firehouse after he'd left the airport on Wednesday, but now he just hurt all over from the physical work. Tomorrow he'd go into the bar and work. He hadn't been there in almost a week. Good thing he had an amazing assistant manager.

He had to keep busy though. Without her here, without knowing what was going on in her head, what she was planning on doing, he had to keep busy or he'd go stir crazy and go get her. Again. Caveman style. It had worked before, but he doubted it would work a second time.

He got up and stripped his T-shirt and jeans off before he padded to the bathroom and a hot shower. Summer might be coming on, but nothing let loose the aches and pains better than hot water pounding on his back.

He groaned in pleasure as he stepped under the spray and simply stood there for a moment, letting the tension ease, letting the knots get worked out under the massage setting, the jetting pulse of the water. It felt almost as good as an orgasm. Almost.

And that thought had him stroking his semi-hard cock to full hardness and length. He hadn't come since Wednesday either, not since he'd screwed her in the truck. Being inside her that one time without a condom nearly did him in. He'd come so fucking close to unloading in her, but he knew he couldn't, not yet, not until they'd come to some understanding, some agreement about the future of their relationship.

His hand on his cock flexed and gripped the shaft tighter, the strokes long and sure. He spread his legs and braced his feet against the inside walls of the shower enclosure, and then he leaned forward and braced his free hand on the wall. The water pounded at the muscles in his lower back and the moan he let go had nothing at all to do with the masturbation of his penis.

Justin closed his eyes and hung his head again, concentrating on the sensations flowing through his body, his mind wandering to Ella and the feel of her in his arms, in his lap, surrounding him in smiles and heated wetness.

He had no idea why he'd fallen in love with her, what it was that had touched him so deeply about her. She was like a fire in his blood and the fact that they'd started out as friends only made him surer than ever that she was right for him, that they were right for each other.

His fingers curled against the tile wall as his orgasm crept closer. His balls started to draw up tight to his body. His fist pulled on his cock harder, faster, working the foreskin over the head. Damn, he loved that feeling just before his sperm erupted from the tip. The all-over tingling. The impending pleasure he would feel from his toes up to his balls, up through his gut and out through his mouth as he groaned, or moaned, or shouted.

Then it was there and his hand was lightning quick over the shaft, his fingers impossibly tight around the hardness. Semen hit the wall and slid to the floor of the shower. Ella's name was a grunt from his lips, a monologue in his head. He swore he could smell her, could taste her. He needed her. Dear God, he needed her.

He let go of his dick and braced that hand on the tile wall as well and took several deep breaths. If he thought he was tired and worn out before, it was nothing compared to the boneless feeling he had right then.

The bed was calling his name, and he wasn't going to waste time getting there. He'd send one more text to Ella before he fell asleep and hope there was something from her when he woke up. He didn't think he could go the rest of the weekend without knowing what in the Sam Hill she was thinking.

Thinking was exactly what Ella was trying not to do. She was failing miserably.

"Clear your mind. Focus on the breath. Breathe in and...breathe out through the stretch."

Yes. She could do this. She really, really could. She could put Justin out of her mind for the next thirty minutes. She had to. He was all she'd been thinking about for days. And well, she was doing it again now. Crap.

"Lift now and lower into Downward Facing Dog. Heels to the floor. Breathe in and...breathe out through the stretch, feeling your muscles lengthen."

Ella followed her yoga sequence. It had become as familiar to her as any of her other daily routines. She'd taken up yoga after her separation and had slowly made her way into Pilates after her divorce. She loved the way the stretching made her feel, the change in the shape of her body and the tone that she felt. She'd lost a little weight and in general felt better in a way that other exercises had failed to provide. Yoga and pilates gave her energy, gave her balance, incredible flexibility and helped her to focus.

Usually. Today was not one of those highly focused days. The previous two days hadn't been any better.

She missed him. She wanted him.

"Knees gently to the floor and lower yourself into Child Pose. Arms stretched in front. Breathe through the stretch. In. Out. Just relax into it."

She tried. She tried so hard, but it just wasn't working for her. Her mind was not centered on her exercise. It was centered on a cowboy five hours away. She'd been half in the moment and half daydreaming of the different positions that would make sex even more interesting than it already was with Justin.

Sex. She couldn't stop thinking about it. She'd been without him for only a couple of days and she wanted him more. She'd gone months without him before, but this time it was different somehow. She could go to him or she could run from him. She was free to make whatever choice she wanted.

And that left her feeling even more uncentered and unbalanced.

The soothing female voice on her yoga DVD, the one Ella usually got lost in as she moved from one pose to another now simply irritated her. It wasn't that voice she wanted to get lost in. She wanted the deep Texas twang whispering in her ear, to slide over on him, to lift into him, to bend forward for him. She wanted those hands, those arms, that body, that man.

"Crap."

Ella lifted out of her pose and crawled to her laptop and turned the DVD off. It was no use trying to focus through the rest of it. She'd be better off getting the rest of her stuff together. She had a couple of hours of work to do before she checked out and headed to the airport.

She pushed the eject button on the disc drive, put the disc in its case, and then dropped it into her laptop bag. Her phone beeped at her with an incoming text message on her way to the bathroom for a shower. Before she picked it up, she knew it was him. No one ever texted her except him, and a small smile crossed her lips.

He'd sent her text messages for the last few days, and though she hadn't responded too much to them, she cherished each and every one. She read them more times than she was sure was healthy, but his words to her meant as much as his actions. She had to make a decision soon about what she was going to do. He hadn't pressured her or asked. He hadn't given her any further prodding to choose him. He'd simply told her he loved her, told her hello, told her he was thinking of her.

She picked up the phone and pressed the On/Off button at the top. Sliding the lock bar down, she pressed the envelope icon on the screen. Sure enough, the text was from him.

Going to sleep. Miss you, baby.

As the previous messages had done, this one made her smile too. He thought about her, likely as much as she thought about him. She really wasn't sure what to make of it. No man had ever affected her like Justin. Was this really what love was? She'd thought she'd felt love before, but this was different than anything else.

She typed him back. *Miss you too. Sleep well. Talk soon.*

She turned the phone off and dropped it in her purse. She'd shower and head to the conference room. There was a test to give, which she honestly didn't understand. Only through experience could they actually master the materials and information they were given. Practical application was the key, but corporate wanted written documentation that employees were present and accounted for, that they were paying some sort of attention to what she was saying.

She'd be happier when the new training system she'd been working on could be implemented. The test system would be up and running in a couple of months, just in time for the new property in Houston to open. The front office staff would take tests on the computers and every ninety days they'd have a quality assurance re-test to take for re-evaluation.

The job made her happy, kept her mind sharp, kept her thinking and experiencing. It kept her occupied until night came and she was alone with her thoughts. Television didn't interest her save for the weather channel so she would know what to pack. She liked to read, and her guilty pleasure was romance novels. However, when she read them, her mind inevitably turned to Justin. She cooked and cleaned and sometimes went out with friends, and the fact that she was alone, that she'd chosen it, wasn't lost on her.

She was still lonely though. That hadn't changed. And honestly, she was tired of thinking about it, tired of living it. She just didn't know exactly what to do about it.

That was a complete lie too. She knew what to do—she just hadn't decided to do it. He was waiting for her and would welcome her with open arms should she show up on his doorstep, but it was what happened next that she didn't know and truth be told, that's what concerned and scared her more than anything.

She'd once heard it said that if you have to choose between two lovers, choose the second one because if you'd really been in love with the first one, you wouldn't have fallen for the second. She was separated, officially, on her way to divorce when she met Justin. She'd thought long and hard about leaving her marriage. Had tried to stay and make it work. Had tried to change who she was even more to make it work. It was when her ex had chosen watching the NFL draft on television over spending some time with her, over pausing the recording for a few minutes, over the nap he'd claimed to need right before he remembered the show he'd wanted to watch that something inside her head clicked and something inside her heart had shut down.

Justin was different though. He'd chosen her and kept choosing her. She came first. Whenever she said she could see him, he never hesitated. Whenever, wherever, however, he would show up, he would give her his undivided attention. But could weekends of sex and lust and hunger turn into a life spent together? Would he take her for granted? Would she do it to him? Would they end up as roommates? God, she didn't want to travel that road again. It was painful and alienating and sad. Sh—

Her phone beeped again, dragging her from her thoughts. She couldn't be happier about that at the moment and pulled her phone from her purse.

You should go without panties today.

Ella's mouth dropped open. She typed back. *I can't do that.*

Why not?

She'd known he was going to ask that as much as she knew he knew what her response would be. *I'm at work.*

So? I'm not saying you have to show anyone.

He had a point. Still, she had planned on wearing a black skirt she'd purchased in a little boutique shop yesterday during lunch, but now she was rethinking that. Would it be best to go without panties if she wore pants instead? She honestly didn't know. She'd never done anything like it.

It'd be sexy and it'd make me happy.

And there it was, that extra little temptation, that extra little nudge. It would make him happy. How long had it been since anyone had wanted her to make them happy? How long had it been since she *could* make someone happy? She didn't know if her husband had ever been happy with her or with anything about their life together. He'd never said, at least not while they were married. Now, yes, he seemed.

So did she.

Okay, but only because you think it'll be sexy. There was no reason to give him a bigger ego than he already had.

Good. Send me a picture up your skirt.

I didn't say I was going to wear a skirt.

So? Wear one.

Dictatorial bastard.

Hey, I remember that word.

LOL. I'm sure you do.

One of their early trivia nights at the bar had included a word game that went from table to table. The rules had been to start the next word in a sequence with the last letter of the previous word. He'd used the word bastard, and she'd used the word dictatorial. The memory made her smile. She'd always loved word games and trivia and Jeopardy. Her ex hadn't been able to stand them, but Justin... He'd made them even more fun for her than usual. He was light and vibrant and quick witted. He could come up with answers or words without thinking too hard and had oftentimes been correct.

Going to sleep. Take me a picture. Call me later.

Okay times three.

Miss you, baby.

Me too.

She turned off the phone and slipped it back in her purse again. The skirt was already laid out on the other bed. The sheer lavender blouse hung in the closet and her black sandals, the new ones with the wedge heel were sitting by the door. She'd bought a new lavender bra and matching panties set, but it appeared she'd been leaving the lacy panties behind.

Another smile flitted across her lips as she wiggled out of her yoga pants and pulled the tank top over her head. Only in private would she wear something like a tank top or such form-fitting pants. She'd lost weight. She'd gained some strength and some definition, but she hadn't gained the confidence needed to go out in clothes that would cling to her curves..

It had been good for her, though, taking up yoga. Until today that is, when she found she couldn't stop thinking of the cowboy in Texas waiting for her. *Waiting. For her.* The thought was novel, but she knew it was true. He was waiting to see what she would do. *She* was waiting to see what she would do.

She turned on the shower and grabbed the vanilla body wash off the marble countertop. Taking a whiff of the sweet-smelling soap, she sighed. She should send for some cupcakes for everyone today. It would be a nice treat for them after the long training sessions they'd had the last few days. Perhaps she'd send out for some coffee too. There was a Starbuck's just two doors down from the hotel.

Her mouth was already watering at the idea of coffee and cupcakes. A quick scrub and washing of her hair, and she was out of the shower in no time, dried and with her teeth brushed before she walked out to get her pan—

"Crap. Not wearing panties today," she muttered as she turned and headed back to the bathroom. Blow-drying her hair didn't take long, neither did the application of moisturizer and a little powder. Digging through her make-up bag for the mascara, her fingers brushed against the small light blue bullet vibrator, and without her conscious mind realizing it, she pulled it out and depressed the small button on the bottom.

The little toy buzzed to life in her hand.

She had gotten herself off each night she'd been in New Orleans, sometimes more than once, as she was unable to keep the thoughts of Justin naked, Justin sliding into her, Justin holding her down, Justin spanking her out of her head. Holding the bullet firmly, she touched the top of it to her right nipple. Her eyes connected with her reflection in the mirror and strangely kept watching as she circled the erect tip. It became firmer and sensitive the longer she teased it. She moved the toy over, never breaking eye or skin contact, to the left breast where she repeated the same slow circling around that nipple. Her breasts felt swollen and heavier the longer she teased and manipulated.

A soft moan escaped and brought her gaze up from her mirrored breast to her eyes. Her pupils were darker, dilated. She lowered her gaze to her lower lips and found them to be redder, fuller than she normally thought they were.

Her skin took on a flush that had nothing to do with the residual steam in the room as she trailed the toy between her breasts to her belly. She drew swirls on her skin around her belly button before taking the toy farther to the top of her mound.

She'd shaved last night and sent up a prayer of thanks for the new shaving creams and gels and lotions that allowed her to shave one night and be baby smooth for the next day or so.

With her free hand, she reached and parted the lips of her pussy. The wetness she found there had nothing to do with her recent shower. It was her constant companion now. It was all because of Justin, all because of the awakening that had taken place in his arms.

She touched the toy to her clit for a brief second before pulling it away again. She slid it through her labia, twirling it through her juices before circling it against her clit again, just around the edges for a moment, for such a brief moment before pressing it and holding it to the tight, hard button.

"Oh."

Her eyes closed and she leaned forward to rest her hand on the counter, bracing herself. The vibrations made her knees weak, the longer she stroked, the longer she pictured Justin in her mind.

He'd like this. He'd like to watch her masturbate for him. He'd like to see her pleasuring herself, getting lost in the sensations. She would like it too, once she got beyond the initial embarrassment of touching herself in front of another person. She didn't imagine it would take her long to get over it though. His effect on her was that strong.

She imagined him standing behind her, watching in the mirror, maybe standing off to the side just a bit. He'd just let his gaze travel up and down her body, stopping to focus on wherever her hands happened to be at any given time.

Her breasts would swell under his stare as they were swollen now. Her legs would get restless and spread a little wider, exactly as they did now. Her gaze would clash with his and then drop, move away from the intensity only to be drawn back by a rough whisper. Only after he had her complete attention tugged and torn between him and her body humming for release would he bid her to watch herself in the mirror again, to see herself as he saw her. Beautiful. Sensual. Sexy.

"Yes," she whispered to his imaginary form.

She pressed the button on the bullet again and the speed increased. She jolted forward, thankful to be braced against the counter. Her legs bent at the knees, and she rocked her hips back and forth as she put more pressure on her clit.

The vibrations drove her, and in her mind's eye, in that place just off to the side of her where he watched from, he lowered his jeans and took his cock in his hand. She loved him in jeans. She never wanted to see him in anything else. Nothing else would look right on those lean hips, cradling his balls, shaping his ass.

He moved his hand up and down the shaft, his thumb and forefinger closing over the head as he pulled up, paused, and then let his fist drift down again. Faster and faster, in time with her own undulations, with her own increased hunger for orgasm, he mimicked her frenzy.

She watched him in her head as she watched her own image through the looking glass. She'd never watched herself masturbate, never watched the changes that came over her as she peaked and fell over the edge into bliss. She'd never seen the pure beauty of her own sexuality until right in that moment. He was the muse for her, the inspiration that tugged her toward the cliff, the voice that urged her to fly over.

"Justin. Justin. Justin." His name was a litany, a prayer, a pleading on her lips. Her fingers curled into themselves on the counter, and she pushed the button one more time with her thumb. The speed rocketed her higher until her orgasm broke through.

It started in her toes—they tingled. It raced up her legs— they also tingled. It flooded her sex with pulsing vibrations making her inner muscles clench tight and release. She didn't let up on the pressure. She just moved the end of the bullet all around her clit, its edges and just below where another jolt of pleasure had her groaning low and incoherent.

The man in her mind grunted his own release and she could have sworn she felt it, could have sworn he was right there with her, sharing the erotic moment instead of just being a figment of her aroused imagination.

She lifted up on her toes and felt the trembling in her thighs, the quiver in her stomach, the release of swollen pressure in her breasts. She sighed as the tail end of the orgasm flowed through her and slowly lowered herself back to the floor and turned the toy off.

She smiled softly at the woman staring back at her and waited to return to normal. Although she wasn't quite sure what normal was anymore. Change was good and she was learning to both like and embrace it, even if that meant she was scared of it at first. Justin was a good example of change. He was young and outgoing. He was a homebody as much as he was a guy who liked to go out and party. He loved his friends, given how much he used to talk about them and he adored his family. He was the life of wherever he was and she was the wallflower.

Maybe opposites really did attract.

Her cheeks were a little rosy, but she needed to get moving. Picking up the toiletries from the counter, Ella went out to the bedroom area of the hotel room and packed up her suitcase. She put some lotion on her legs and arms before she slipped the skirt up her lower body, zipping it on the side. She tried to ignore the fact that it slid over her bare behind with a soft caress and simply focused on the fact that it swished around her knees. It was one of the things that had prompted her to buy it. She loved light, flowing, swishy skirts.

Next, she put her bra on. With her yoga over the last few months, she'd actually gone down a size, but her breasts were still a bit on the big side. A double-D was something she'd be glad to keep though, especially with her trimmer waist and leaner hips and legs. She liked the difference in her body and knowing there was a man out there that found her irresistible... "The cowboy ain't too damn bad himself," she said into the room.

After zipping up her suitcase and tugging it to the floor, she took her blouse from the hanger in the closet and slipped it on. It was soft and cool against her skin and she couldn't help but wonder what it might feel like without a bra under it. She could only do such a thing in private, but imagined it would tease her nipples to exquisite hardness.

She stepped into her shoes as she buttoned her shirt, and then took one final look in the mirror, this one full length outside the bathroom door. She looked professional and even a bit well sexed. That thought brought a sly grin to her face. Well sexed indeed. Who knew masturbation could make a woman feel that way? Certainly not her, at least not before this moment.

She'd always masturbated, but had to keep it a very private thing when she was married. Her ex hadn't liked the idea of it, had issues about it from a very old-fashioned upbringing, so she'd kept it to herself, usually when he wasn't at home or when she was in the shower, times when she knew he wouldn't walk in on her.

Staring at herself, she pondered the things that were a part of her past but that had shaped how she felt and looked at things in the present time. She had been married. She had dated before she'd gotten married. She had lost her virginity in her teens, and she certainly hadn't been a prude of any kind. She'd lived and experienced things, but something about right

144

now, right then, had a profound effect on her and the direction of her life.

She figured she would always learn new things about herself, but at the same time realized it didn't mean she couldn't be content or happy along the way. Nor did she have to do it alone if she didn't want to. She had someone who would hold her hand when she wanted, someone who would hold her up when she needed it and someone to just talk to her.

She hadn't been sheltered, but the last few months sure as hell felt like waking up from a very long sleep. She smiled at the woman in the mirror again, and then grabbed her purse and laptop bag. She'd come back for her luggage after class was over and head to the airport, hoping she'd make the right decision when the time came. It was time to put up or shut up.

Justin slammed his hand on top of his phone. The damn thing was ringing. He lifted his head and with squinted eyes, tried to focus on the clock. Shit. He'd been asleep for almost seven hours. Sure as hell didn't feel like it. The phone started ringing again, and he flopped back down, his heart kicking up speed in the hopes it was her. A quick glance at the screen showed it wasn't. Damn.

He pushed the button to talk. "Yeah?"

"We got that shipment of beer today, and I don't have the time to go out there and inventory it."

"Didn't think it was supposed to get here until tomorrow?"

"Wasn't. But it's here now and taking up space. I'm doing good on my own in the bar, but can't leave it. The Saturday night crowd is bound to pick up soon. I need you to come in and deal with the new stuff."

"All right. I'll be in in about thirty minutes." He scrubbed a hand over his face and smothered a yawn. "Make that forty-five."

He turned the phone off and waited for the home screen to show itself. No messages from her either. Shit. He tossed it to the bed and slid out to scan the room for a pair of jeans. He wasn't in the mood to care what he looked like so long as it was right about even with presentable.

"I bet she went back home. Damn woman is gonna drive me insane." Finding the pair he was looking for, he stepped into them. "She's gonna make me go get her again. This time I will use the fucking rope and tie her ass to the bed."

Grabbing a shirt from the closet, he shrugged into it and snapped it up the front. "Not the pretty green rope either. Nope, going to use the rough stuff on her. Teach her to make decisions that aren't good for her. Keep her from running away."

Hands through his hair to smooth it out from sleep, and a brushing of his teeth, he grabbed his boots from beside the head of the stairs, along with a pair of socks and headed down. Coffee would have to wait until he got to the bar. Or hell, maybe he just needed to go ahead and pop the top on one of those fancy new beers they'd just gotten in. He hadn't tried blueberry beer yet. Might be good. Might wash away the grumpy taste in his mouth.

She needed to learn that he was good for her—that she had nothing to fear from him. Damn woman.

Keys in one hand, wallet and sunglasses in the other, and he was out the door. Shit. The phone was still upstairs. Oh well. If she called, she could damn well wait until he got home.

"You got up on the wrong side of the bed, huh?"

"What're you doin' here?" he groused at his younger brother.

"Takin' care of the horses and the cattle that had strayed to your side of the ridge. Been workin' my tail off while you've been catchin' your beauty sleep."

"Oh piss off, man." There was little to no heat behind his words, but the sentiment was sound. He didn't want to be teased or joked around with. The more he thought about Ella and the shit she was putting his heart through, the grumpier he got. The problem was if she'd only open up and let him in, maybe he could help with whatever fear she had. He knew she wasn't doing this on purpose to try to hurt him and he hadn't gotten to the hurt stage yet, but too much more of this uncertainty...

"How'd things go with your girl?"

Justin shrugged and shook his head. "Great until she left. Now she's thinkin' too much."

"How do you know that?"

"She always thinks too much. She wants to know everything is going to work out the right way this time instead of the wrong way again."

Joe started coiling the rope he held in his hands. "Maybe she doesn't want to make this a real, everyday, permanent thing. Maybe she just wants to keep it long-distance. You know, a weekend fling instead of somethin' more. You are kind of a pain in the ass to be around all the time."

"Maybe," Justin said absently, his mind turning its wheels over those same thoughts. He wasn't willing to hedge those bets yet. It was still a wait and see thing. If she went back home to Alabama, they were going to be havin' a come to Jesus talk about their relationship. Not that he was religious by any stretch of imagination other than to make Ella scream the good Lord's name when she was riding wave after wave of heavenly pleasure.

Shit. He was such a sap and so head over heels for that woman.

"I got a bit more to do 'round here. You headed into the bar?"

"Yeah. New shipment of beer."

Joe nodded. "I'll be headed in soon to the feed store. That mare is going to give birth any day now."

"Doc been out here?"

"Other day while you were gone. He said Mable is doing fine, just got to keep an eye on her and then make her as comfortable as possible until he can get to us."

"Okay. Well, when you get done at the store, stop in the bar. We need a guinea pig for the new beers."

"Oh hell, no. I ain't tryin' no fancy-dancy fruity crap that someone's passin' off as beer. Just gimme a Bud."

Justin gawfed out a laugh. He sort of felt the same way as Joe, but he was at least willing to give it a try. "See ya."

Joe nodded and the brothers each turned in different directions. Justin was half tempted to go back to the house for his phone, to see if she'd sent a message yet or not, but he didn't. He just kept walking to his truck. He'd know what she was up to sooner or later, and if she wasn't coming back, he'd just rather know later.

Chapter Nine

Ella took a deep breath and straightened her skirt and blouse for about the tenth time since she'd stepped up on the porch. Who knew it would be so hard to do this? Who knew she'd be so damn scared? He wouldn't reject her or turn her away, so why was her heart pounding and her body breaking out in a cold sweat? Why was uncertainty curling in her belly?

When he'd come to get her and she left with him, she hadn't been scared at all. *Because you just thought it was another weekend in bed with him and this is different.* The voice in her head was right. Didn't mean she was happy about it, but she'd been going in the same circles with him for too long. Change was good. She knew this, believed it. It was time to put that belief into practice and embrace this particular change.

She raised her hand to knock, but the voice from behind stopped her.

"If you're lookin' for Justin, he's not here."

Ella turned and came face to face with a younger version of her boyfriend. Boyfriend? Lover. Justin was her lover. Boyfriend implied... But didn't lover imply...? Ah, hell. She focused on the man in front of her. This one looked just as good as Justin and then some. Must run in the family. "Do you know where he is?"

"They needed him at the bar for somethin'. You Ella?"

She nodded. "I am."

He grinned, and in that moment, he could have been Justin. He took his Stetson off and slicked his hair back in a gesture that made her ache because it was so close to what Justin had done the other day when he'd poured water over his head. She had it so very bad for her cowboy.

"We were beginning to think you didn't really exist. Our folks have been anxious to meet you. I'm Joe, by the way."

"Nice to meet you." She didn't know what to say to the other comments he made so she just took the steps down from the porch to the ground. "Maybe we can remedy that sometime, meeting your parents, I mean." She extended her hand, and his larger one wrapped around it.

Up close, his eyes were more hazel than Justin's green eyes. He had a bit of blond scruff on his chin where Justin's would be brown. "Can you tell me if he'll be back soon or where the bar is? I really need to see him." *Before I lose my nerve altogether and just head home.*

He settled his hat back on his head. "I take it he wasn't expecting you to show up?"

"No, he wasn't. We hadn't... Well, I hadn't said..." She had a hard time putting into words that she'd once again left the man's brother without an answer.

"I don't know when he'll be back, but I'm sure he wouldn't mind you goin' on inside to wait or I guess if you want to go up to the bar, I can take you. I need to head in that direction anyhow."

Did she really want to do this in a public place? "That'd be great, thanks."

"Good. Okay. I'll go 'round back of the stables and get my truck."

Ella tried not to groan when he turned and walked away. His ass in those jeans reminded her of Justin's ass. Wasn't she a sight? Ogling the second brother while the first one was every other thought she had. Though, if both of them stood side by side, facing away from her, she'd have a really hard time telling the two of them apart. Especially if they both wore cowboy hats. They were as close to identical twins as she'd ever seen without them actually being twins.

She waited and tried to ignore the doubt running circles inside her head. She was firm in her resolve to give the relationship with Justin a chance. And it was a relationship. It wasn't just sex, wasn't just a weekend fling, wasn't just an online, distance thing. It was a relationship, and she needed to treat it as such. He deserved that. Hell, he deserved better than that.

The rumble of a truck reached her ears before she saw it come around the side of the house. She smiled. It was the red truck Justin had driven to New Orleans the first time they met outside Birmingham.

Ella climbed up in the cab, and Joe started them down the long dirt drive to the highway. She'd only been gone for four days, but it felt like longer, except for the lingering aches in her body when she moved certain ways.

"You love my brother?"

The question caught her off guard. Neither of them were looking at each other, but she felt his complete attention just the same. Did she love his brother? Yes. Was she ready for his family to know it? Was Justin ready for his family to know it? Okay, well yes, he probably was ready for that.

"It's okay if you don't. At least not yet. He's not always an easy guy. Jus' the way he talks 'bout you sometimes, the way he got so excited when he was goin' to see you and then the way he was kind of a pain in the ass when he got back. I know he cares about you. I 'as just wonderin'."

"Yes, I do love him."

"You here to tell 'im that?"

"I've told him once already, but yeah, I'm here to tell him that."

"Good." Joe nodded and tapped his fingers on the steering wheel. "Yeah, that's real good."

Ella looked out the window. White fences, brown fences, horses, cattle, ranches. There was green grass everywhere, wild flowers along the side of the road, and she rolled down the window, letting the fresh air blow across her face. Of course, the smell was kind of hard to take in a few areas, and she was thankful for the ability to hold her breath for a bit.

Joe was on the other side of the cab laughing. "I 'as thinkin' you might not want to be doin' that, but I guess livin' in the city, you're not so used to country air."

Ella relaxed and laughed with him. She'd never had siblings and her parents had been so unhappy in her early years that she'd grown up much more serious than a kid should have to. Justin had once told her she didn't laugh enough. He was right about so many things that she didn't doubt he was right about this too. "Something like that. It's so open out here, so pretty and peaceful. I can see why Justin loves it so much and why he doesn't really have a desire to leave."

"I 'spect he'd leave for you."

"I'd never ask that of him."

"Prolly wouldn't have to ask. He'd just do it."

She didn't disagree but she didn't want that on her shoulders. Justin loved his home as much as he loved anything. He wanted her to love it too. It was part of the reason he'd insisted on bringing her here last weekend.

"Let's hope it doesn't come to that." And it wouldn't. Not if he gave her any say in it. Her job was flexible enough with her traveling that so long as she had access to a major airport, she could work from anywhere.

He turned to the left off the highway to a main street area. On one corner was a diner. On the other was a feed store with a number of pickup trucks backed up to it. Down a bit from the diner was a general store complete with rocking chairs out front filled with old men. It was like a scene from a painting. How pretty and perfect it was. How lively. This straight-out-of-the-past town was full of people. Where'd they all come from?

"You look a little dumbfounded," Joe said from beside her.

"I am."

"The town's name is Crooked Creek." He pulled into a parking spot in front of a... Was that a saloon? It had wooden, swinging doors like one and, judging by the music coming from inside, it sounded like one. Would she find Justin in period costume? Would there be saloon girls with frilly skirts and corset tops?

"It's a great little town, and it's one-hundred-percent modern. Internet, phone, satellite sports packages on the television for football and basketball."

"It looks so old," she said as she got out and shut the truck door behind her.

"It is. Most of it from the eighteen hundreds. It's been completely rebuilt in places, refurbed in others. There's old money 'round these parts. The owner of the bar, Bo, well, some relative of his from way back pretty much owned this town. It had died out when folks started movin' more toward Dallas. It was a ghost town for a long time, just sittin' here on the side of the road. There used to be a creek that ran back there in the woods toward a lake. Both are dried up now, but in some places you can still see the bed and how it twisted this a way and that. That's how the town got its name."

Ella nodded. There would have to be money to revive a western town like this. "How did it come to be like this?"

"When Bo came back from the first Gulf War, they wouldn't let him go back to being a cop, so he took the money he had saved and started board by board rebuilding. Pretty soon, others started helpin' once they realized what he was up to. It took a couple of years to get it up and running. It's been bustlin' ever since."

"And Justin works here?"

"Yep, and the firehouse is a couple streets over along with a couple of bed and breakfast inns. Those are much newer than the buildings on this street. Of course, if you want a big chain store, you need to head closer to Dallas, but even those places aren't too far away. 'Bout another fifteen- or twenty-minute drive."

That's where they'd stopped for Starbuck's on the way to the airport a few days ago. This little area was a step back in time at first glance, but as she stepped up on the wooden walk and pushed through the saloon doors, she saw exactly how twenty-first century it really was.

Light fixtures made to look like replicas of gas lamps were electric powered. A jukebox poured music into the room. Tables gleamed, though the floor was scuffed from many years of use. It was an eclectic mix, and it meshed in a way she hadn't thought it would or even should. At the same time, she was well aware she didn't know anything about interior design and what should or shouldn't go together.

A guy at the bar looked up at her and then behind her. Joe must have come in as well.

"Hey, Bo. Justin in the back?"

"Yeah."

Bo looked from her to Joe and back again. "She Justin's girl?"

Justin's girl? Had he been talking to everyone about her? No one she knew knew anything about him. Not her friends, her family, her boss, no one. Well, the ones from when she worked in the front office of the downtown hotel knew of him from trivia nights, but she hadn't let on to them either, that she and Justin were sleeping together now.

"Yep. Mind if she goes to see him?" Joe's hand pressed against the small of her back and nudged her forward. Over her shoulder, he pointed straight ahead toward another set of double wooden doors. "Go right through there. He should be in the storeroom or on the loading dock."

Ella nodded once and took a few shaky steps, entirely and uncomfortably aware of Joe and Bo watching her. She didn't dare look anywhere else for fear there were other eyes staring at her as well. She hadn't meant to cause any kind of attention to be drawn to herself. She didn't even take time to calm her thundering heart or take calming breaths or give herself a pep talk. Not like she had before Joe had come upon her on the front porch at the house. No, she just went through the doors and came face to butt with Justin.

He was standing up on the tailgate of a truck, bent over, digging in a box. His ass and her face were literally at the same height. The urge to swat him was strong and just as she raised her hand to do so, he stood straight and turned to jump down.

Her face was now level with his denim-covered cock. She dropped her arm, swallowed hard and licked her lips. A whole other trail of thoughts were swimming through her head now, and she had other urges building up.

"Bad girl," he laughed. "I'm up here." He jumped down when she didn't immediately lift her gaze to his face. His fingers touched under her chin and raised her head up. "Good to see you, baby. I wasn't sure I expected to."

"Joe brought me."

"Will have to thank him. But I meant, back here in Texas. I thought you'd go on home."

"I didn't."

"I see that. Why not?"

"The sky." It was the first thing that had come to mind that didn't seem to be any kind of threatening to her emotionally. She knew she was going to have to get over her fears, but one step at a time.

"The sky?"

"I want to see it again. Full of stars and a big, bright moon."

Justin nodded and smoothed her hair over her ear. "And just where would you like to see it from?"

"The swing in your yard."

"Alone?" His hand slid around the back of her neck and up into her hair where he lightly sifted the strands through his fingers before tightening them into a fist and tugging.

Ella lifted her eyes up to stare into his. "No. With you."

"Good answer," he whispered just before his lips touched hers and his arm yanked her hard against his body.

Their tongues met and slid and collided against one another. Her hands fisted in his button-down shirt as the direction of their heads changed so they could deepen the kiss. The arm at her back slid down over her ass and pulled at the fabric until it was bunched up and she felt air flowing between her legs.

"We can't do this here," Justin whispered into her mouth and proceeded to kiss his way down her throat to the center of her chest. His teeth went to work on the buttons of her blouse.

"Then we should stop." *Please don't stop. Please, please, please don't stop.* Looking around, there was no one. She didn't see anyone walking around, and she didn't know where the owner of the truck Justin had been on was. She didn't think Joe or Bo or anyone else had come outside either.

And it was Justin. She couldn't stop if the place was set on fire. She wanted him way too damn much to stop. She wiggled her ass where he had her skirt bunched in his fist and he groaned, tearing at her blouse. She heard the rip but didn't care.

"No panties."

"You said not to," she panted.

"Uh-huh. Yep. I did." He stood to his full height and looked into her upturned face. "But we still can't do this here."

"Where can we?"

He laughed and shook his head. He let go of her skirt and tried to repair the damage to her shirt, frowning when he realized he couldn't. It was well and truly torn. "Don't you ever stop thinking about sex?"

"Evidently not when it comes to you, but then again, you started it."

"Maybe I should look into getting you some counseling."

"Maybe you should look into getting yourself inside me."

Justin raised a brow and smirked. "Demanding little wench. When did you get so damn bossy?"

Ella pouted and lowered her eyes to focus on the toe of his boot. "I don't know. I just get horny around you."

"But why so much that you can't think straight?"

157

She huffed and tried to move out of his hold. He wasn't having any of that and backed away, pulling her with him until she stood between his legs when he took a seat on the truck's tailgate. "I don't know, Justin. Honest, I don't. I just... I sometimes feel that if I don't... I feel like I need to..."

"Let it out, Ella. I'm not going anywhere, no matter what it is."

He wasn't. She knew that. She believed it with all her heart and yet she still found it hard to let him in. His eyes were more gray than green today and were calm and tender. His touch was too. She liked it. She hadn't liked soft and sensual for so long, hadn't had it for so long. "I don't know how else to be. I don't know how to just enjoy being touched without becoming so frenzied, so impatient."

"I love touching you, baby. I love hard, rough sex. You know I do. I sometimes like it slow and sweet, though. I need both and maybe you do too, even if you don't think so."

He wasn't completely wrong about that. "I told you to go and get ugly if you didn't want me gawking at you all the time."

"Is that really part of why you're so impatient when we get together? Because you like the way I look?"

"Sorta. You're gorgeous to me, Justin. You're young and hot. Every woman who knows you must think the same things I do." She fiddled with the snaps on his brown checked shirt. He was the only man she knew who could pull off that kind of checkerboard print and still be sexy as the devil. Well, maybe Joe could. "I don't know why I need it hard and rough and possessive. I don't know why I need to be taken like that all the time. I just do. I need it." She hoped he could see and feel the urgency in her eyes, her voice, her tense body language. She didn't know how to convey it any other way.

He tilted her chin and kissed the tip of her nose. "I know. I'll give it to you as much as I can, but sometimes baby, you'll have to let me touch you soft and gentle. You're gonna have to let me love you. I'm not goin' anywhere and neither are you." He pinned her with nothing more than his gaze. "Are you?"

For a moment, all she could do was stare at him. Was she going to leave again? Was she there to stay? Did he even know how hard it was for her to want to stay? "No, Justin. I'm not going anywhere."

His grip on her chin tightened and he growled... Actually growled before his mouth took hers again. This kiss was hard, insistent, plundering. It stole her breath, her senses, her very sanity in its violent heat. He gave her exactly what she wanted and she grinned in her mind, answering him with the same violent need flowing through her, but then his kiss changed, softened. He still held her chin, but his grip gentled. His lips caressed rather than demanded. His tongue coaxed rather than took.

It was a genuine kiss of love, of pleasure filled with promise. He could show her desire and let it curl and build and fill her, but could she let him? Could she let him give her that and not get bored with it herself? That was the real fear. She'd always gotten bored before and drifted away until there was nothing left.

Justin lifted his head, his eyes heavy with need and hunger. She understood it, recognized it as the same need and hunger flowing through her.

"What's wrong?"

"I get bored. Soft and tender and sensual and slow. I get bored. I thought..." She looked at his shirt, focused hard on the shiny little snaps. "I thought if I kept you at arm's length, if I kept us distanced, then I wouldn't get bored and end up hurting you." She looked up, afraid of what she might see reflected back at her. There was nothing but solemn understanding. He really was too damn good to be true, yet there he was, as real as she was. "When we'd meet, it would be so hot and frenzied and we couldn't keep our hands off one another. It kept it exciting for me and kept me wanting more and now..."

"Now you're afraid if we make this some sort of permanent relationship, where we see one another a lot, that you'll get bored sexually and want to move on?"

Ella nodded.

"Oh, baby." He pulled her in for a quick kiss, and then lingered for a moment. He touched his forehead to hers. "I don't intend for you to get any kind of bored. We have enough kinks between us to last years and years. Trust me. And if you ever start to get that feeling, come to me, talk to me and believe in me enough to shake up your world again."

She did believe in him. Despite her own fears, if she didn't believe in him, she wouldn't be standing on the loading dock behind a bar outside Dallas, Texas. She'd be at home in Alabama instead, curled up on the couch, eating crappy food and watching even crappier movies about love and happily ever after.

"I know you're scared. I know you think this will turn out like your marriage. It won't. I'm not him and you're not the same woman who married him or divorced him."

"How do you know?"

He looked confused for a moment. "How do I know what? That you're not the same woman? Easy. You're here. You came to me instead of going home."

Ella thought about it and realized he was right. She couldn't be the same woman that nine months ago had divorced her husband. She'd changed a lot and she'd changed not only outwardly but inwardly too. It hadn't been until he'd pointed it out that she'd even realized it.

She nodded and looked at him. Their faces were level with the way he was sitting on the tailgate—his hands were loose on her hips, her fingers were smoothing out his shirt where she'd bunched it up during their kiss and after. "We'll try it."

"Damn right, we'll try it. We'll make it work too. Nothin' worth havin' is ever easy."

"Especially me?" She smiled, teasing him.

There was a roll of his eyes and a quirk of his lips before he eased her close for a sweet, soft kiss. "Most especially you."

"What do we do now?"

"We let me get finished working here, and we let me take you home."

Brow furrowing, she started thinking again. "How are we going to do this, Justin? I live in Alabama. You live in Texas."

"No idea, but we'll work it out. I promise, baby." He eased her back just as gently as he'd eased her forward.

She took a couple of steps so he could stand. She couldn't *not* worry about it. Worry was her middle name. It's one of the things she really liked about him. He didn't worry. He was easygoing, took things as they came, and when they didn't come on their own, he took action and went to get them. He had the patience of a saint, but only to a point. She guessed everyone had that limit they were willing to go to before they'd had enough. She never thought she'd had it but evidently she did too.

First her marriage, now Justin. "Are we moving too fast?"

"Too fast?"

"Well, yeah. I mean, I've only been divorced... Well, less than a year." Not too many more months and it would be a year, but she wasn't going to remind him of that.

"And?"

"Isn't this too soon? Shouldn't we be taking it slower?"

"How much slower do you want to take it?" He stood to his full height from where he'd been bent over going through a box of beer. "We saw one another for a weekend every other month, sometimes every month. Until last weekend, I hadn't seen you for two months. It's not like we've spent every day together."

"We talked just about every day or emailed."

"Not the same thing, baby, and you know it."

She did, but the fear made her question it all. "But then because we haven't spent a lot of time together, may—"

He had her pinned against the wall before she could finish her sentence. His tongue was in her mouth, his hand loose around her throat, his leg pushed up high against her bare and *sans*-panties pussy. He rubbed at her mound with his thigh until she was moaning and kissing him back, clutching at him, sliding herself against his jeans, her heels leaving the ground.

He tugged his mouth away, across her cheek, to her ear, where he nibbled on the lobe around the small purple dangle of her earring. "Now listen to me very carefully, Ella."

She nodded and felt his lips curving into a smile. She couldn't believe how turned on he had her within seconds. She hadn't even been thinking about an orgasm when she'd protested how much time they should have spent together, but now it was all she could think of. His hand at her throat, his knee between her legs. She was balanced on his thigh and held up between him and the wall and both were immovable.

Her arms hung limply at her side, and her mouth was suddenly dry. But her pussy, dear God, it was soaking wet. There would be a trail of her juices along the faded denim of his jeans when he dropped his leg to the ground. There'd be no way to hide it. Everyone inside the bar would see it. She groaned and ground herself against him harder.

She evidently liked that idea. She liked knowing that everyone would know what they'd been doing. Well, maybe not know for sure, but they could at least suspect. Only one of his jeans legs would be wet and she'd probably still have that dazed look on her face—that one she'd had back in the mirror in the hotel.

"You listening, baby?"

"Yes," she whispered around the cotton in her mouth.

"Stop trying to borrow trouble for us, okay? We'll be fine if you'll stop worrying about how much or how little time we've spent together." He bit the whirl of her ear. "I know intimacy scares you. I know you think I'm gonna do to you what he did, ignoring you and not caring enough to ask about your day. I know you think there's something wrong that you like it rough and hard like this. But stop. Let me show you that this can be and is different. I'm gonna take such good care of you, baby. I just need you to trust me and stop worrying. You're here—give it a chance."

With every word he uttered softly, he was rubbing at her, holding her at the hip, driving her forward, upward. She heard what he was saying, every syllable, every inflective nuance, but the arousal was high and pointed and she was right on the edge of the cliff.

He pressed her clit hard with the edge of his knee when he stopped speaking, and she buckled, gripping his shirt at his sides as the orgasm pounded through her. She saw stars behind her eyelids. Stars in the bright light of day. Heat suffused her body from the tips of her toes to the top of her head. Her pulse throbbed beneath his fingers, and she'd have given anything to be stripped naked and fucked against that wall right then and there.

He let her ride it out, let her keep it going as long as she needed. And she needed... She gasped when his hair brushed her chin and his mouth settled just under her jaw. She felt the edges of his teeth and then he was sucking at her skin.

She jolted again and another small gush of come soaked into his jeans.

Leaning her head back against the wall, she opened her eyes and tried to focus on her surroundings. The first thing she saw was the blue of the sky, the pickup and Joe. Joe was standing just on the edge of her vision, but she saw him just the same.

She tapped Justin on the shoulder. "We have company," she whispered brokenly against his hair before turning her head as far as she could with his lips and teeth still attached to her neck.

Joe was smiling. Well sort of half smiling, half smirking. She felt her face heat and couldn't help the moan that slipped out when Justin's tongue licked at the spot he'd just been nibbling on. He laughed and lifted his head, kissing the tip of her nose before turning and looking at his brother.

"Somethin' catch your attention?"

Ella tried to push at Justin's shoulders, but he didn't budge and he didn't remove his knee. He kept her pinned against the wall, kept his chest pressed against hers, kept flexing his leg against her pussy. She had no recourse other than to stay, to calm down, to relax and let happen what was going to happen. He did however remove his hand from her throat, but not completely. He stroked the side of her neck, pet her hair, caressed her face with his fingertips.

It was designed, she knew, to keep her in the moment, to remind her that he was there, that she wasn't alone, that this was part of what turned him on, being naughty and sexual in public. He liked extreme public displays of affection and evidently displayed in front of his brother didn't bother him. His touch and the way he kept her from moving away without her making a scene was his way of helping her to be comfortable with it rather than be embarrassed by it.

Joe glanced from Justin to Ella and back again. She couldn't read the expression on his face. Amusement? Arousal? She couldn't read his eyes either.

"I'm done at the feed store and came to see if she needed a ride back to the house."

A ride. She needed a ride all right, but not back to the house.

"Appreciate it, but no, I'll take her myself. I won't be here much longer."

"Okay." His eyes focused on Ella. "It was nice to finally meet you."

Ella tried to keep from blushing, but she knew she hadn't been successful by the wink Joe tossed her way. "Likewise," she managed, though she wasn't quite sure how around the large boulder lodged in her throat.

"Now where were we?" Justin asked, his full attention turned to her after Joe went inside. He touched the sensitive skin where her pulse beat beneath. "Should I give you a mark on his side too?"

"No." Though, her sex clenched and screamed yes.

"You sure? I'm not sure your body agrees." He leaned down and licked a trail from the hollow of her throat up to that pulse point.

The man was more than she could handle, and she wasn't sure how she was ever going to get enough of him. She wanted him all the time. Even as her body calmed from her orgasm, it immediately began to heat again, preparing for another one.

To her relief—or disappointment—he let her go. She used the wall to brace herself until she could steadily move away from it.

"You need a drink?"

Yes, actually. Can I have that entire case of beer you're checking out? "Maybe some water."

"Bo has cold bottles behind the bar."

"You think he'll mind me asking for one?"

"Not a bit, but I'll go get it for you."

"I can get it for myself." She started to walk inside but stopped. "Justin? Do you think he heard me? You know, earlier?"

"I imagine he did. Hell, I imagine everyone in the bar did."

Ella groaned and closed her eyes. "Great. Just great." She pushed through the doors and moved toward the bar slowly, one foot in front of the other. Bo looked up. If he'd heard her come on Justin's leg outside against the wall, his face gave no indication of it. He smiled kindly at her.

"What can I do you for?"

"Justin said you had bottles of water." Even though his face didn't give anything away, did hers? Could he tell she felt embarrassed?

"That I do. Just one?"

"Two if it's not a problem." Did her voice give it away? Or was she just paranoid because she wasn't used to public displays?

"Not at all."

She took the bottles and turned away quickly. She had half her bottle empty by the time she got back to Justin. He was unloading another case of beer from the truck and looked up when she handed him the extra bottle.

"Thanks, baby. I'll be done soon and we can go."

She took a seat on the corner of the tailgate. When she looked down to adjust her skirt, she caught sight of the small tear in her blouse from Justin's teeth. She had completely forgotten about it, but from her angle, she could see the hole and directly onto the skin between her breasts.

"Sorry about that. I didn't mean to rip it." Justin was looking at her as he took a long drink.

"I know."

"You want to get something to eat before we head home?"

Home? Where was home? With him? And where with him? Texas? Alabama? "Not unless you do."

Even though she'd rationalized that she could live anywhere because of the travel nature of her job, she wasn't sure she wanted to live just anywhere. She didn't know where the best place for her or their relationship was. He was right in that things needed to change and that they needed a fair chance, but where?

"No, I'm good to go back to the house and clean up. I've got plenty of food there to feed us." He finished off his water and capped the bottle, his gaze trained on her. "What are you thinkin' so hard about now?"

She smiled guiltily. "How this is going to work," she replied honestly, again. "We live in two separate states."

"We do." He spun away and knelt on the ground to inspect the beer. "I'll go to 'Bama. Look for work, a place to stay."

"You wouldn't live with me?"

"You're not ready for that."

She wasn't. He was right. "Joe said you'd offer to leave Texas for me."

"Yep."

"I can't ask you to do that."

"You didn't ask. I volunteered."

"What if you can't find something for work there?"

"Then we talk about you coming down here."

"You're very accommodating."

"I'm very much wanting a relationship with you. Compromise, sacrifice, give and take. It's all part of it, and I'm willing to do whatever I have to in order to make it work."

Exactly how many times was she going to make him say it? Not those exact words really, but repeat that same sentiment? "I know." And she did. She just had to make sure he knew she was willing to do whatever it took as well to give them a fair shot. "How about this solution? I move here. I see about leasing my place for what? The summer? I'll get a little place somewhere around here that isn't too far from you, and we work on things."

He whipped around and leveled a stare at her. "Yeah? You'll do that?"

"Yeah," she said without hesitation. "I'll do that. We both know it'll be easier for you if I do." They also both knew, without speaking it aloud, that it was the hardest thing for her to offer. She could offer her body no problem, her mind too, but leaving

168

her comfort zone, moving close to him, opening herself up to the deepest kinds of intimacy on a normal, everyday basis was the hardest thing for her.

"I know a place, and you could move in immediately."

"Okay." Her heart was pounding clear up into her throat. She wouldn't, couldn't back out. Justin was special and deserved her openness, her willingness. The grin that broke out on his face told her everything she might ever need to know about how this was going to work from there on in.

"We should seal this deal with a kiss. C'mere." He crooked his finger at her.

She stood, curious about the look on his face, one she couldn't describe. Sort of smiling, sort of lusty. Almost lecherous, and for a moment, it gave her pause. What was he up to? She stopped in front of him and reached out her hand, thinking he would take it and stand himself. Only he didn't.

He kissed the palm of said hand and placed it on his shoulder, and then dropped to both his knees and dove head first under her skirt, planting his mouth at the top of her mound and sliding his tongue down through the lips of her hot, wet, very needy pussy.

Parting her legs allowed him to deepen the kiss and he braced her with an arm around her hips. As kisses went, it was the best one so far for sealing deals and one type she could get used to when it came to agreeing on things.

Ella lifted her skirt in one hand and looked down. Something about the sight of his dark head between her legs... She twisted her fingers in his hair with her other hand and held on tight. Pleasure arced through her and her knees started getting weak. She held fast though. She didn't want him to stop, didn't want to break the contact.

At this rate, he'd never get done with the beer inventory.

And at this rate, with his tongue doing wicked things to her, she didn't think he cared about finishing the beer inventory.

Epilogue

Three months later...

Ella loosened her grip on the slats in the headboard. He was driving her insane. I.N.S.A.N.E. He was only as far up her body as the back of her right knee and she was ready to scream. She hadn't gotten any better at the slow, sensual lovemaking in the last three months than she'd been at it in the months and year previous. At the same time, it didn't mean Justin was giving up or stopping. No, at least once a week, sometimes twice a week, he was killing her softly and tenderly with whispers and strokes and caresses.

"Admit it, baby. You love it," he mouthed against her thigh before he took a little nibble. It was only meant to tease and not inflame.

"I will not admit anything," she replied, grumpy and aroused and so ready to fuck it was ridiculous. That was the crux of the matter anyway. He'd spend hours licking and touching and it did indeed arouse her to the point she was writhing and nearly crying by the time he sank deep inside her.

She didn't love it. She didn't hate it either. And she'd never, ever admit that his tenacity in this was one thing she'd grown to love most about him in the months she'd been living in Texas. He never gave up. Not on anything, and most definitely not on trying to seduce her into slowing down sex and slowing down her mind.

That he kept at it, kept at her, kept her wet and hungry and so needy for him when he did this, kept her on the cusp of orgasm, didn't hurt.

"Should I start on your other leg?" he asked, nipping at her ass cheek.

"You should get naked and have sex with me." But truth be told, they both knew how much she loved being naked while he was still in his jeans and boots. Something about the rough-and-tumble way he looked and the scratch of the denim against her smooth skin.

"Point taken."

And he was gone, down at the foot of the bed, lightly tickling her foot with his tongue. Ella groaned and dropped her face into the pillow. "Justin, please..." she whimpered, bordering on whining.

"I am pleasing, baby."

She'd just gotten home from a trip to Houston and this was the first time she'd seen him in about four days. Phone sex, sexting and just his normal sweet texts kept her company and she'd been so ready to get back to him, back to dinners and movies and trivia nights at the bar, back to the swing in his backyard.

"That's it. You're relaxing."

His hands kneaded her calves and up the back of her thighs. Where his mouth traveled, his hands followed. She tried to spread her legs, tried to hint at where she really wanted his mouth and his hands, but he held her firmly in place.

She squealed in frustration into the pillow, and then sighed when his fingers started to massage the tension from her lower back. If she let herself, she could get so used to this treatment, this pampering, this gentle, indulgent side of him, of them.

She turned her head. "That feels amazing. Please don't stop."

"Not gonna stop, baby," he murmured, moving to straddle her legs.

He eased up on the pressure in his fingers and lightly grazed her sides, down to her hips, and up to the sides of her breasts. It was a different touch, one that had her melting boneless into the mattress while arousing her to a point of almost not being able to stand it. She needed to come. If he'd just let her come, he could take all the time he wanted touching her.

His cock rubbed against her ass crack every time he moved. She tried to lift up, tried to wriggle around, but he was having none of it. The smack to her right butt cheek was nothing if not deserved.

"Calm yourself. You're not going to get anything until I'm good and ready to give it to you."

Dammit. And in her head, she stomped her virtual foot in a fit of frustration. "I know."

"Then why do you fight me? You know your body likes it. You know as well as I do that you're so juicy between your legs that there's likely a little wet spot under you where you've leaked on the sheets."

Oh yes, her body did like it. Her body liked it every time he touched her—in whatever way he touched her. She closed her eyes. "I don't know." But then again, maybe she did know.

"Stubborn girl. You just can't let go of the fact that all your worries haven't come to pass." He leaned forward, his chest against her back, his mouth at the side of her face. "Things between us are so damn good and I know that most of the time you know it, you feel it. It's just these times when we're quiet and I'm making love to you this way that you start getting all defiant."

"I don't want to be."

"Then don't be."

"Easy for you to say."

"I know." He kissed her cheek and trailed his lips along her jaw. When she tilted her head and gave him access to her throat, he took it.

Ella moaned as her body erupted in goosebumps, and she shivered in pleasure.

"See? Not so bad to give in to it."

"No," she whispered. There never was anything bad about giving in to it, giving in to him.

"One day, you won't fight it. One day, you'll come to me begging for it, begging for me to just lay you out and play with you."

As he kissed his way around to the back of her neck and down the ridge of her spine, Ella tried to imagine what that would be like, pleading with him to do exactly as he said. Strip her down, lay her out, and just play with her. Giving herself over to it was one thing. Asking for it was quite another.

He reached her lower back, dipping his tongue into the twin dimples. "Pull your knees up under you. Don't spread open, just raise your ass in the air for me. Yep, just like that." He lightly kneaded the flesh of her bottom, stroked over the curves of her hips and thighs before spreading her cheeks.

His warm breath heated already warm and moist skin. He exhaled the hot air against her and involuntarily, the muscles surrounding her asshole tightened and pulled in. He chuckled behind her before she felt his hair tickling her and his tongue licking, flicking lightly at sensitive tissue. Again, she squeezed, though this time she wasn't sure whether she did it or her body did it without thought.

It wasn't exactly what she wanted, but damn if she could find a reason to complain. It felt too freaking good. Only one other lover had licked her ass, had rimmed her with his tongue or finger, and that first time she'd nearly come off his bed and the orgasm it had sparked was akin to an explosion in every cell of her body.

That Justin was doing it, that this man she was head over heels in love with was doing it, she couldn't even begin to imagine what the orgasm would be like. She was aroused for him before she ever... Well, she was always aroused by him, for him, because of him. Her pussy was always wet. Her breasts were always just slightly swollen in anticipation of his touch, his look, his mouth. Her ass always quivered in the hopes of a swat from his hand. Everything was about him, and if she thought she was aroused before with his light touches and caresses and teasing licks, it was nothing compared to the fire sliding through her blood now with his tongue pressing against the opening to her ass.

"Keep hold of the headboard and spread your knees for me," he murmured between stabbing licks.

Ella again did as he told her. As she opened, wetness slid along her pussy lips, seeped against her thighs. Heated wet flesh suddenly touched with the cool air in the room made her moan.

"See, just as I suspected. There's already a wet spot on the bed." He *tsked*, and then moved away slightly.

In the small space of time until he returned his tongue to her ass, she felt exposed, alone, bereft. She hated that feeling, especially when there was no cause for it. He wasn't going to leave her like that. He'd never leave her like that, unattended and unfulfilled. But then she heard it, the buzz of the wand, and that last night before she'd left for New Orleans months ago filled her.

Just as soon as he'd switched it on, he switched it off. "Justin?" Her voice quivered and the muscles in her legs started to twitch at the memory of the orgasms.

He switched it on again and edged it closer to her until she could feel the energy coming off it. He hadn't touched her with it yet, but the anticipation was just as powerful.

He switched it off. "Do you remember that night, baby?"

Ella nodded, not sure she could speak again, though she tried. "Y-yes." Her voice sounded more like a squeak.

"I tied you up and took away your choices about the wand. I forced those delicious orgasms from you, didn't I? Until you sagged against the ropes and could barely talk."

She nodded once more, unsure where this line of conversation was going and part of her didn't even really care. She only wanted whatever he had planned for her. She was very ready, very willing, and hopefully very able to take it too.

"I'm not going to do that this time."

Ella whipped her head around until she could look at him. His chest was sweaty. His eyes were dark and heavy lidded. His body was primed and on edge, much like hers was, yet, different.

She watched as he shook any kinks from the cord where the wand was plugged into the wall beside the bed. She watched as he slid the wand up toward her, and she lifted a questioning brow. He smiled.

"That's right. You're going to do it this time. You're in charge of these orgasms. I'm going to be quite busy, and you, my love, are going to come until you can't take it anymore."

Her? He was giving her the wand? She already knew how powerful it was but also knew that had he not held it to her before, she would have pulled it away after the first or maybe second, but she wouldn't have been able to give herself more. The painful tenderness of her clit would have stopped her. Justin on the other hand, just kept giving her more, pushing her harder.

She'd loved every second of it.

With a shaking hand, she reached out for the toy. It was heavier than she'd imagined it to be, but then, he'd been holding it before.

"Go on, baby. Turn it on. Feel its power travel through your arm."

She flipped the switch on and felt exactly what he'd said. Power. It made her whole arm vibrate and the tighter she held it, the more it seemed to vibrate through her. And that was just on low. She turned her head to look at him. He simply nodded his encouragement. His smile was sweet and lusty, his body tense with hunger because his eyes said so. She'd learned a lot about him by the looks in his eyes.

She shifted on the bed until she'd worked the head of the wand between her legs. His fingers wrapped around her wrist and tugged a little more then he pressed until she felt the rubber of the toy against her clit. The fingers of his other hand flexed against her ass and the deep grunt he let loose sent shivers through her body.

"Hold it tight and push it hard against your pussy. Trust me. You can take it."

His breath was hot between her legs, hotter than the humid heat she was creating all on her own. His fingers still covering hers, he urged her thumb against the switch. The rotating head started spinning and Ella jolted. "Oh God, Justin," she squealed.

One dip of his tongue into her sex and then it was gone, as were his fingers. He replaced them on her ass and spread her wide again, his tongue attacking her dark hole.

Those sensations combined with the spinning wand head... But it still wasn't enough, yet.

She sucked in a breath and tensed, flipping the switch to high. The orgasm hit her immediately and she grunted. It wasn't delicate or pretty. It was animalistic and primal. And it was ongoing. His tongue didn't stop and neither did the wand. She didn't pull it away, she didn't stop, she didn't ease up on the pressure. She kept it up, kept it hard against her pussy. She wanted more.

The tingles started in her toes, it was a slower come this time but not by much. Another orgasm crashed over her and she couldn't catch her breath before yet another one was upon her and come slid down her thighs.

Her throat was dry as she gasped for breath. Her mind couldn't form a coherent thought save for the word "more". She kept wanting more and more. The pleasure was just one peak after another. There were no endings. And then he was inside her, his cock pushing into her clenching channel, forcing himself against the resistance of her muscles.

He groaned behind her and started thrusting. Hard. Powerful. His rough hands scratching against her hips as he held her fast against his fucking.

"Keep going, baby. Give me more."

She nodded. Or at least she thought she did. She wasn't sure anymore what she was physically doing. Her whole body was trembling, shaking, cresting. The wetness continued and leaked out around his cock. Messy. He'd always liked messy, dirty sex. She did too. God help her, she did too.

That thought brought the next orgasm through her. The cry she emitted was more like a croak, and then it was just one long moan and tears fell from her eyes.

"Can you give me one more?"

Justin leaned forward, reached around and beneath her to hold onto the toy with her. His strength picked up where hers left off, and he ground the wand into her abused and thrilled clit. She bucked against the orgasm, somehow harder than the rest and on the edges of consciousness, heard him yell and go still behind her.

He turned off the toy and moved it to the edge of the bed. She didn't know if he was done emptying inside her. She was trembling too much inside and out to know which tremors were hers or his. He still held her, was still hard inside her, was still with her.

"Let go and lie down. I've got you," he whispered into her hair, urging her gently with his body.

She did as he said and slowly stretched her legs out and let her body fall to the bed. She groaned at the aches in her muscles and joints, and she couldn't stop twitching. He was on top of her back with his cock buried inside her, and his fingers twined with hers up by her head.

He nuzzled his face against her neck and shoulder and for a few moments or a few hours, she had no idea how long, they lay there like that. She might have drifted in and out of sleep, but he was there when she came to, his lips trailing against her skin.

"Ella?"

"Hmmm?"

"I love you, you know."

Another round of goosebumps covered her skin at his words. But then, those words from him always had that effect on her, along with the butterflies in her belly. Her heart ached with how much she loved him, how deeply in love with him she was. "I know," she said, her voice husky and sounding not entirely her own. She was going to need a drink of water soon, but she wasn't willing to give up this comfort for anything right now.

"Your lease is up on this place soon."

"Yes." It was only supposed to be for the summer as was the sublet on her apartment in Alabama. That had been their deal. She would rent a place for the summer and they'd see where and how they were doing at the end of it.

"I want you to stay."

He'd never asked before. He'd inferred it, hinted at it, assumed it even, but never had he come right out and said the words like that. She wanted to stay. She wanted to keep going with him, like this. Her job was going well and her relationship with him was more than she ever imagined it might be. Was it because they didn't live together that it was still fresh and new and happy? Was it because they didn't see each other every day because of jobs that either took her out of town or kept him at the firehouse for a few days at a time? Or was it just because they loved one another, that they talked to one another, that she could tell him anything, say anything, ask for anything, even his attention?

She didn't know what it was. Maybe they were just meant to be. "I want to stay." He pushed up against her and deep inside her and flexed his thighs against hers, making his cock flex against her walls. He let out a sigh and she smiled.

"But are you going to?"

"I don't know if I can do another three months on my apartment. The email I had last week said the couple wanted to know if we could extend for six months."

"Give it to them. Give them six, nine, twelve. Turn it all over to them. Move down here, baby."

"I don't know that Millie is going to let me have the apartment here for another three months or so."

He squeezed her hands and nipped at her shoulder. "Don't act like you don't know what I'm saying."

She knew exactly what he was saying and deep down it was what she wanted, but... "Spell it out, Justin."

"Move in with me."

Happiness settled inside. "I'd be all twisted up in your life," she said softly, squeezing their hands.

"Yes, and there's nothing I want more than that. Move in with me, El."

Ella closed her eyes and took a deep breath. It's what she wanted too. She wanted to live with him out on that pretty ranch in that cute house. When they were both available, they practically lived together anyway. Either he was staying at the little apartment he'd found for her upstairs and two doors down from the bar, or she was staying at the ranch. Nothing was ever official though. She'd only brought clothes and a few personal items. Her furniture was back in Birmingham.

She'd taken a big leap of faith in herself and in them by moving for the summer. He'd not let her down, and she'd been happier than she'd ever been in all the years of her marriage. It might not work out with Justin in the long run, in the forever sense. Then again, it might. It really, really might and she really, really wanted it to.

There was only one way to find out... "Yes."

About the Author

To learn more about Lissa Matthews, please visit www.lissamatthews.com. Send an e-mail to Lissa Matthews at lissa@lissamatthews.com.

The second time around is even sweeter...with cherries on top.

Sweet Caroline
© *2010 Lissa Matthews*
Blue Jeans and Hard Hats, Book 1

Buck doesn't do personal projects. Until he runs into a woman wandering the aisles of the local home-improvement store, looking lost and confused. Just the way this fantasy looks at him nearly buckles his knees. In a hot second, the successful owner of a contracting company becomes a simple handyman, ready and willing to get as personal as the lady will allow.

Since her less-than-golden marriage to the local golden boy ended, Caroline's declaration of independence includes her own business, road trips...and nipple piercings. Now it's time to cut the last tie to her old life, but the house needs some work before she can unload it and move to her dream cabin in the mountains. Hard as it is to admit, she needs a little help.

Over the next few months, he shows her his toys, like hammers and drills, and she shows him hers—like floggers and paddles. And their attraction is the tinder that could send Caroline's plans for an independent life up in flames...

Available now in ebook from Samhain Publishing.

Enjoy the following excerpt from Sweet Caroline...

A five-year age difference wasn't much, but to a woman of forty, it was enough of one to make an impact. Buck hadn't come on to her, flirted with her or touched her unless it was necessary. The only thing he'd ever done to make her think he saw her as a woman rather than a client, was that look of heat every so often when she licked her lips or curled her hair back behind her ears to keep it out of her face. She didn't know if he'd seen the strands of gray at her temples or if he realized she had to use extra creams to keep the lines and wrinkles down to a minimum. But he wouldn't deny there'd been something about her he liked, that brought out that bit of lust in him and it was *that* look he'd give that had her wanting to feel sexy and younger, even if she didn't look it.

"Not a lot of work. I have a couple of baskets to put together, but they don't need to go out until the end of next week."

"That's good. I know I like being busy and seems like you do too."

"Yes. I'd rather be busy than twiddling my thumbs all day wondering what to do. I used to do that far too often when I was married."

Buck leaned his hip against the axe handle, and she had a hard time keeping her eyes trained on his face. She wanted to look down or lean against him. She wanted to drop to her knees, press her face to his crotch and rub her cheek against his cock.

When he licked *his* lips after taking another swallow of coffee, she looked away, somewhere over his shoulder. His tongue licking the drop of coffee seemed to have the same effect on her that it had on him when she did it. And things were even hotter between them after yesterday and last night. She'd not had so much sex in one night in a long while and though she should be sore, all she could think about was getting naked with him again.

She liked feeling free and sexy and pretty and wanted. She liked being the woman inside and letting her out to see the light, to be seen by a man like Buck. Even though he likely didn't know it, he'd helped her to see that side of herself, and she was enjoying the discovery.

She hadn't felt that way about herself during her marriage. At least not the second half of her marriage. When Derek focused on her, on them, she'd felt like the sexiest, most beautiful woman alive, but when he'd started looking away more, wanting and having other women, she lost that feeling. She'd retreated into a shell, and she was damn glad to be out of it.

"That's right. You didn't work before."

She looked at his face again, briefly raising her gaze to his. "No. I started my gift baskets after the divorce. Since it's an online business, I can move it anywhere there's Internet and shipping. I like it and it's..." She shrugged.

"Yes. A personal touch is lacking these days. I've seen some of what you do. It's good. I'm sure your clients are very happy."

Caroline smiled. She liked him being proud of her. "Thanks. Well, I guess I should let you get back to work." She didn't want to though. Staying, talking, looking at him was what she wanted to do instead. The taste of his come was still on her tongue from breakfast when he'd told her to strip down and suck him, and she was eager for him to tell her to do it again.

"Welcome." He picked up the axe, wrapping his hands around the wood shaft and lifted it to rest on his shoulder. The move pulled his tee shirt tight across his chest, and she knew his gaze followed hers as she looked him up and down, smiling into his face and bright blues. "Neither of us wants to work right now, do we?"

Caroline shook her head. "No."

"What do you want, sweet Caroline?"

"More of you."

"Huh. Interesting." She followed Buck into the shed. "I think that can be arranged. I had a thought yesterday about you and this sawhorse here." He patted the piece of wood. "But it might be a little chilly this morning."

"Coffee warmed me up. Didn't do that to you?"

"Oh I'm warmed up, but it wasn't me I was concerned about."

"Sweet of you." Caroline pulled her sweater off over her head. "I'm okay though." And from the way his eyes widened... "Like it?"

He reached out and flicked the ring in one of her nipples. "Love it. You need to wear that kind of bra all the time. Leave those beauties free and exposed."

She grinned. "Yes. Exactly what I was thinking. I have two others, but, there are a host of colors I haven't ordered yet."

"Well, we should definitely get that done. God, Caroline, they're beautiful." He wrapped his large hands around the globes of her breasts and squeezed, tugged, massaged the creamy flesh. She moaned in need, and he grinned at her. "Matching thongs?"

"Lacey boyshorts."

Buck groaned and she purred. "Driving me crazy, woman."

"That's the whole idea," she whispered into his hair when he lowered his head and licked at the valley of her chest. Her fingers unsnapped and unzipped her jeans, and she shimmied out of them.

Buck stepped back a couple inches and looked down. "You deserve a spanking for being such a tease."

"Mmmm." She kicked the jeans off to the side near the door. "And how am I a tease?"

"You came out here under the pretense of bringing me coffee."

She watched him unbuckle his belt and pull it through the loops, one at a time. The hissing sound it made caused her to shiver. "But I did bring you coffee."

"You did."

"Am I to be punished?"

"Spanking isn't for punishment. It's strictly for pleasure. Mine...and yours."

She liked that. A lot. "Then what?"

"You will bend over the top of the sawhorse, spread your lovely legs and have your pussy plundered."

There's only one man she needs to believe in. Him.

If You Believe
© *2009 Crystal Jordan*
Unbelievable, Book One

When it comes to her love life, the name of Aubrey Mathison's coffee shop says it all: "Bean There, Done That". There's only one harmless man in her life right now—the homeless one parked outside the shop. Except the crazy things he says keep coming true.

She has to laugh at "You'll meet your soul mate today", though. Divorce taught her that men as gorgeous as sexy police chief Price Delacroix are not to be trusted. She's totally up for a one-night stand, but more than that? No, thanks.

Price bears his own scars from the past, but he knows instantly that Aubrey is his. How to convince her he wants more than to be her personal jungle gym? Cut her off. That means no more mattress gymnastics—until she starts seeing things his way.

Aubrey is just as determined Price's campaign to wear down her resistance is going to fail, no matter how wickedly determined he is. Until her resident prophet spouts a new prediction: her soul mate's life is in danger...

Available now in ebook from Samhain Publishing.

Enjoy the following excerpt from If You Believe...

Mr. Crazy Man was back. He hummed a little before speaking again. "Dogs are bad luck for you today."

Shit. She hunched her shoulder and spun away. "Thanks."

If she went her normal route home, she'd have to pass by the dog park that made up a corner of the town square. Maybe she would try a different way. Just for the change of scenery. Change was good for the soul, wasn't it? If she went by the dog park, it just seemed like too much self-fulfilling prophecy.

Taking a left off the main path where she usually took a right, she wandered into the older district of town that had great Victorian houses. She'd always loved that style of architecture, but Scott had wanted modern. Now that she lived alone, it just seemed like too much upkeep. And maybe it was because she was afraid it would put her one step away from crazy cat lady to rattle around in a big old house like that. She turned the corner on to her street. She had four blocks left to go.

"Woof." Her blood ran cold at the deep bark that came from behind her. A lot of people walked these streets in the evening. And took their dogs with them.

A kid of about twelve had lost the leash on his Great Dane. The air went whistling out of her in what might have been a high-pitched squeak.

It wasn't that she believed Jericho or anything, but the fire thing had kind of creeped her out. Watching that pony-sized excuse for a dog running at her made her blood run cold. Anyone would freak out. It had nothing to do with Jericho's warning. Nope. Not a thing.

She backpedaled as fast as her legs could carry her just the same. The back of her ankles hit something that yelped and the next thing she knew she was going down hard on the pavement. Her back arched when her tailbone made sharp contact with the ground and all the breath rushed out of her lungs. Curling into a fetal position on her side, she wrapped her arms around her knees and tried remember why she didn't want to die right then.

When she opened her eyes, a pointy little muzzle snapped in her face as a dachshund yapped. Dog breath, *blech*. She groaned and pushed into a sitting position. A strong arm wrapped around her back to cradle her against a wide chest. *Price Delacroix.*

"Don't move, Aubrey." His deep voice rumbled, and that was all it took to get her hot and bothered. Her sex dampened at the sound of his rich, deep tones. The way he smelled. The hardness of his muscles against her body. *Thank you, Jesus.*

"I'm fine." She tried to pretend the breathiness of her voice was just from having the wind knocked out of her. The way her nipples tightened and her muscles softened told her it was a lie.

"You took a hard fall. Stay there." His words were almost harsh, but his touch was gentle when he brushed her hair away from her face. She fought the urge to lean her cheek into his palm. Everything about this man made her react.

Her original assessment that the two of them were destined to burn up the sheets was dead on. She really wanted to try him on for size. She'd bet he fit just fine. "I'm really all right, Chief."

"Price. You'll call me Price." His other arm slid under her bent knees and lifted her as he stood.

She squeaked and clutched his shoulders. His soft T-shirt bunched in her fingers as she held on tight. "Don't drop me."

A wicked grin flashed over his face before he focused on her eyes. Some of her panic must have shown because he cuddled her closer. "Not a chance, sugar."

"Is she all right, Chief Delacroix?" Mrs. Chambers, the biggest gossip in town, reined in her wiener dog and stared at the two of them.

"Oh, she's fine. Ma'am." He dipped his head in a nod, dismissing the older woman while he turned to walk up the driveway in front the big Victorian on the corner. She sighed in envy when she saw it.

She glanced over his shoulder at Mrs. Chambers. An avid gleam entered the older woman's eyes as he mounted the porch. Pitching her voice low, Aubrey had to warn him. "Look, I know you're new in town, but Mrs. Chambers—"

He nudged the front door of his house open, and then kicked it shut behind them. "Will spread it all over town that I carried you into my house? And will probably embellish it by saying that I practically stripped you on the sidewalk and fucked you against the street lamp."

She ran straight into love's arms...
and he isn't letting her go a second time.

Passions Recalled

© *2010 Loribelle Hunt*

Forbidden Passions, Book 2

When his mate and his father died in a freak accident, Jason Leonidas left home and became a park ranger in the Florida Panhandle. The distance and solitude suit him. After all, the less he cares, the less he hurts.

As a hurricane bears down on the coast, he races to secure and evacuate the park before conditions worsen. Just as that point of no return passes he discovers an injured and unconscious visitor. Celeste Lykaios, his mate...who died over a year ago.

Truth has turned Celeste's world upside down. Not only did her family lie to Jason about her survival, they lied to her about his abandonment. And the new boyfriend she'd trusted is trying to kill her. Her only hope was to race into the teeth of the storm to find Jason. She almost made it.

As she and Jason unravel the betrayal that split them apart, the ragged strands reconnect, forming a fragile hope that their love can be salvaged. Out in the storm, the killer waits for a chance to make Celeste the stunning finale in a plan to over throw the Lycan alpha...

Available now in ebook from Samhain Publishing.

Enjoy the following excerpt from Passions Recalled...

There were jackhammers in her head. Even moaning hurt. Funny, she didn't remember partying last night. She frowned, and it made the pain worse. Actually she didn't remember last night at all. Rolling over, she pressed her forehead into the pillow and was immediately swamped by Jason's smell. *Oh, God.* Where was she?

She couldn't think past the pounding behind her eyes, but when the room shook with a crack of thunder she jerked her head up, wincing for her trouble. She hated storms. There was one window, and outside it a palm tree whipped back and forth.

Definitely not in Kansas anymore. Or Atlanta. Whatever.

Rolling back over, she took stock. Her head hurt like hell, but everything else seemed fine. Only one way to know for sure. Gingerly, she pushed up on her elbows, cursing the pounding headache that spread over her face with the strain. She sat up, gasping, and looked around the room. To call it bare was generous. It contained the bed and a dresser. The walls were empty. There was nothing to identify its owner but the scent of the sheets on which she lay.

But that didn't make sense. She looked out the window again as another gust of wind buffeted the house. Rain tapped the roof, and she cocked her head, pressing her hand to the side that throbbed the most. The sound echoed loudly in the room, and her headache seemed to pick up the rhythm, pulsing in time to the rain. It was familiar. Tin would be her guess, and that at least helped her narrow down her location to probably somewhere in the South where in recent years tin roofs had become all the rage. She wasn't sure if she was relieved or disappointed. Not the Southwest, so not Jason's home. She swung her legs over the side of the bed and set her feet firmly on the floor.

And why the hell was she wearing a bikini?

Only one way to find out, Celeste.

She had to venture out of the room, find out where she was and who else was here, if anyone. Her mind refused to accept it might be Jason, even if her body thrummed at the thought. She didn't dare wish it was so. She squeezed her eyes shut. Jason was over. Jason was the past.

She stood and took a step toward the door, but froze when a black leopard appeared and blocked the space. Her eyes filled with tears.

The first time she'd seen Jason in leopard form, she'd been very confused. His brothers looked like typical leopards in their were forms, tawny and gold with black spots. Jason was dark, his coat black, his spots brown to cream colored. He'd explained that sometimes nature threw a genetic anomaly out there, in the leopard *and* wereleopard worlds. Melanistic leopards were often born in litters with regularly colored siblings, probably an evolutionary advantage for jungle ranging leopards. All of the big cat species had melanistic or black versions. The same held true for werecats. Black was not a common color to see, but not rare either.

Looking at him now, she remembered the pain of that conversation. His pain. She'd felt his loneliness and had wanted to soothe it. He'd identified himself as the outsider in his family, but she'd seen how much they loved him, how much they needed and respected him. Although, none of that had really mattered to her. She'd thought he was beautiful. She'd loved him beyond reason. She should have known better, she thought bitterly with the benefit of hindsight, but the observation didn't make one damn bit of difference in her reaction.

He padded closer, stalking, and she clenched her fists. She would not reach out and bury her hands in that fur, would not give in to the tears threatening to fall. The big body pushed against her, his head butting and rubbing against her thigh in a show of affection, and she couldn't help the sigh that escaped. He pushed her until the backs of her knees hit the bed and she sat, giving in to the temptation and sinking her hands in his pelt.

Soft. Silky. So, so dark and lit with light at the same time, like the mysteries of the midnight sky. And definitely Jason.

She was afraid to speak, afraid to shatter the spell. It was the best damned dream she'd had in over a year.

He moved closer, sat on his haunches and rested his front legs along her thighs. Then he licked her, a long swipe of his tongue up the side of her face, over her old scars. The raspy stroke woke memories. This tongue, this man. Months alone and lonely and heartbroken in a hospital bed. Yet she shuddered as her body responded to him, recalled the out of control feeling of being in his arms.

Memory shattered the dream.

Except it wasn't a dream, was it? She pushed against the cat and scrambled back on the bed. Shifting, the man followed, crawling up her body and pinning her under his weight. A growl rumbled deep in his chest.

"No," he ordered, refusing to allow her to retreat.

She tried to push him away, but he grabbed her wrists and held them next to her head, while forcing her thighs apart with his knees and settling between them. His erection pushed hard and throbbing against the juncture between her thighs. She grew slick, felt the swelling in her clit and saw by the way his nostrils flared he knew it too.

"So long," he muttered, before his lips descended on hers.

God help her, she couldn't resist. She opened her mouth to him, accepted the stroke of his tongue. His pelvis ground against hers in a matching rhythm, and she was positive the only thing keeping him from plunging into her was the thin fabric of the bikini. It wasn't much of a barrier, and she wished he'd throw it away. She'd toss it herself if he ever let her wrists go.

The kiss was all too short as he broke the contact and trailed his lips along her jaw, down her neck, and finally closed over the old mark on her shoulder. He nipped it lightly and her back arched, her pussy flooding with cream as an intense orgasm froze her. God, she couldn't respond to him like this, so quickly, after so many months absence. It was mortifying, and she strained against him. She needed a minute to collect herself, to attempt to build some kind of barrier around her heart. She feared she was too late. Maybe she'd never managed to do it in the first place.

He released her wrists, rolled onto his back and moved up the bed, pulling her across his chest with one arm around her waist. Somehow during the move he removed the bikini bottom. His cock insistently pressed against her center and with his eyes he begged for admittance, but he was leaving the choice to her. How could she resist? Her body had been dead for a year and now it screamed for the fulfillment only he could give her.

Refusing to acknowledge the niggling worry over where he'd been or where she was or even if it was real, she sat up on her knees and moved over his hips. She held her breath, closed her eyes and allowed the fantasy to take over as she took him inside her. Slow. So slowly. If this was a dream she didn't want to ever wake up.

She felt his hands behind her neck, over her back. Shivered at the sensation of fabric sliding free of her skin. He was finally seated all the way inside her, when his hands closed over her breasts. Her entire system threatened to melt down.

"Look at me," he demanded.

SAMHAIN
PUBLISHING

www.samhainpublishing.com

Green for the planet.
Great for your wallet.

It's all about the story...

Romance

HORROR

www.samhainpublishing.com

CPSIA information can be obtained at www.ICGtesting.com
Printed in the USA
BVOW071303191012

303459BV00005B/6/P